Niall doesn't have a problem with shifters, but can anyone blame him for not trusting them entirely? It has nothing to do with who they are, but rather with the fact that the pride has been in hiding for too long—okay, and maybe it's because both his best friend and his dad are dating shifters, and he's kind of jealous.

Billy didn't mean to become a runaway groom. Instead of marrying his long-time boyfriend, he's back in his childhood room in Green Hill, and he has every intention of hiding there as long as he can.

But Billy's mom is dating someone, and while Billy is happy for her, he wishes he could avoid the man's son, Niall. Niall is rude and doesn't let Billy forget he almost ran him over with his car—he was overwhelmed, all right?

There's no ignoring that Niall is Billy's mate, though, no matter how much Billy wishes he could. Finding his mate is the last thing he needs, especially when Niall is the grumpiest man he knows. Can he ignore their bond, though? And even if he wants to give this a try, will Niall?

Niall
Copyright © 2021 Catherine Lievens
ISBN: 978-1-4874-3219-5
Cover art by Angela Waters

Published by eXtasy Books Inc or
Devine Destinies, an imprint of eXtasy Books Inc

Look for us online at:
www.eXtasybooks.com or www.devinedestinies.com

NIALL
GREEN HILL PRIDE 4

BY

CATHERINE LIEVENS

CHAPTER ONE

Niall's father was hiding something. Niall had no idea what it was, but he wanted to find out. He *needed* to find out because he wasn't ready to lose his father, and he was afraid he might.

He couldn't stop thinking about it. After losing his mother ten years ago to breast cancer, he was terrified of something similar happening to his father. It would be just like the man to hide health problems from his children to protect them, even though all three of them would be angry. The fact that Niall's father was hiding something pointed to that, and Niall had no idea how to find out what was happening. He knew his father, and if he pushed, his dad would clam up.

"Watch out!"

Niall just had the time to crunch forward. He felt something move above his head, and he stayed still until he was sure the danger was gone. When he straightened and turned around, he found his best friend glaring at him.

"I told you I was coming in with this," he said, gesturing at the beam of wood he was carrying on one shoulder.

Niall hadn't heard him. If he was honest, he had no idea what was happening around him, which was a problem, considering his job.

He sighed and rubbed his face. "I'm sorry. I didn't hear you."

Val stared at him for so long that Niall wondered if he was going to try to hit him with that beam. Instead, he put it down, even though Niall was pretty sure that wasn't where the beam was supposed to go. Val didn't seem to care, and he came toward Niall, peering at him. "What's going on?"

Niall shook his head. "Nothing." He had nothing to say, not when he didn't know what was happening to his father.

"Bullshit. Something is going on, and I'm getting worried. Usually, you wouldn't hesitate to tell me." Val paused. "Unless it has something to do with me?"

"You're not the center of the universe."

That made Val smile. "Simon would disagree."

"That's because he's smitten with you."

"I would be worried if he wasn't, considering he's my mate."

Niall had hoped Val was done interrogating him, but he should have known better because he continued.

"You'd tell me if something was wrong with you, right?"

"You're my best friend. Of course I would." And Niall should probably talk to someone about this. The best people to do it with would be his siblings, but he was closer to Val. "Maybe we can talk after work?"

"We should, but you have to survive until then. It's not like you to be distracted."

"I promise I'll be more careful." If Niall's father really had health problems, the last thing their family needed was for Niall to get hurt.

He did his best to focus on the work once he and Val were done talking. Luckily, they were in charge of this team, so no one had anything to say about them taking a five-minute break to talk, especially after the way Niall had been behaving. Niall was pretty sure most of the team was worried about him, and he made an extra effort to focus on the work and on his coworkers instead of obsessing over his father. Whatever was happening, there was nothing Niall could do right now. Worrying wasn't going to help, and his father would kick his ass if he found out that Niall had been so distracted he'd almost taken a wooden beam to the head.

Niall was relieved when it was time to take a break. He let Val talk to the owners of the house they were working on today and started a quick clean-up. He wasn't in the mood to talk to anyone, even though technically it was his job, since his uncle owned the company he and Val worked for. His uncle had always liked Val best when it came to the job, though, and Niall didn't mind.

"Okay," Val said when he got back to Niall. "What's going on?"

"Not here," Niall murmured. He didn't want the customers to overhear a personal conversation.

Val nodded. "How about we grab something for lunch? I'll tell Simon I won't be home until tonight."

"He won't care?"

Val beamed, just like always when he spoke of his mate. "He's not my jailer. He loves me, and he understands I have other people in my life, including you."

Niall was relieved Simon hadn't demanded Val stop being friends with him or something like that when they'd bonded. Niall had been wary when Val found out he was a shifter's mate, and he still was. Niall had no idea what to expect when it came to shifters, at least not in real life. He knew the theory, just like everyone else, but when it came to his best friend, it wasn't enough.

There was nothing he could do about it. Val knew that Niall wasn't sure how he felt about shifters, but he hadn't considered that when he'd decided to bond with Simon. Niall hadn't expected him to. Val was an adult, and he knew what he was doing better than Niall. Besides, he was happy with Simon. The relationship between Val and Niall had changed since Simon had become part of Val's life, but then it would have changed even if Simon hadn't been a shifter and if Val hadn't been his mate.

"Let's grab something for lunch," Niall agreed.

Val was already texting, no doubt telling Simon that something was wrong with Niall and that he was going to try to get information out of him.

Niall didn't mind, although he wasn't sure how he felt about Val telling Simon what was going on with him.

Niall realized it was his fault he didn't know Simon well yet. Simon and Val hadn't been together long, but it had been a couple months, and he should know his best friend's mate better than he did. He needed to change that, but not right now. Now, he had to focus on his father, and Val might be able to help.

They drove to the diner separately, each of them taking their own truck. That way, once they were done, Niall could head back to work while Val visited Simon for a quickie or whatever he was planning.

"What's going on?" Val asked once they were seated at a table, both of them holding a glass of water.

Niall took a sip, trying to put how worried he was into words that made sense. Val knew Niall's family, and he would be worried, too. Maybe there was no reason to hide the fear. "My father is hiding something," Niall said.

Val blinked. He waited for a moment, maybe for Niall to continue. When Niall didn't, he frowned. "What's going on with Regan?"

"I don't know. That's the problem. He's been acting weird, and I know he's hiding something."

"But you don't know what it is."

"That's what scares me. What if he's sick and doesn't want to tell us?"

Understanding dawned on Val's face. "You think it's cancer?"

"I don't know. I haven't tried talking to him yet, but it's obvious there's something he's not telling us. He's not answering his phone as often as usual, and he's also not calling as much. I went to visit him the other day, and he wouldn't let me in. He was flustered. He said the floors were wet, but he was only wearing sweatpants."

"Maybe he was doing something, and he didn't want you to find out."

Niall grimaced, understanding what Val was implying. "Maybe." After all, his father was an adult, but Niall didn't want to think about his father in relation to anything sexual. "But mom died ten years ago. He would have been doing that even before now. No, this is a recent change."

"How recent?"

"I don't know for sure. I realized about a month ago."

"And you've been keeping that to yourself until now?"

Niall shrugged and took another sip of water. "You had other things to focus on. You just moved in with Simon, and you're still in your honeymoon period. I didn't want to bother you."

Val reached out and slapped the back of Niall's head. "You wouldn't have bothered me. This is your father we're talking about. I want to find out what's happening. I care about him, even though he's not my father."

"I know, but I don't have anything else to tell you. I have no idea what's going on."

"You should talk to him, and Flynn and Shona. It involves them, too. Whatever your father is hiding, if it involves his health, they need to know."

He was right. Niall should have talked to them before now, but he hadn't wanted to worry them. He was going to have to, though. This was a family matter, and they needed to be involved. "I'll text them to see when they're available. We can get together and talk about this before we confront Dad."

"Exactly. Maybe they know something you don't. Maybe you're worrying for nothing."

Niall hoped Val was right, but he couldn't dismiss the niggle of worry and dread that had hooked itself in the back of his mind. He'd already lost his mother. He didn't know what he would do if he lost his father, too.

Billy was doing the right thing. Or maybe not—at this point, he had no idea what the right thing to do was. He only knew that he was freaking out and that he had to get away from everything, including Robin.

God, Robin. He was going to hate Billy after this was over, and Billy wouldn't blame him. He would even stay still if Robin wanted to hit him, although he suspected that wouldn't be the case. It wasn't the kind of person Robin was. But Robin would be destroyed, and even though Billy knew that he couldn't find it in himself to turn around and go back to his boyfriend.

Or was it ex-boyfriend? Ex-fiancé? He and Robin had been supposed to get married about half an hour ago, but instead of joining Robin and marrying him, Billy was on the run.

He snorted at himself. He couldn't believe he was a runaway groom. He really should have thought better before he actually got to his wedding day. Now that it was here, he was panicking, and the only thing he could think about was reaching Green Hill. That was where he'd grown up and where his mother still lived. She would be able to help him.

Except she wouldn't, because she was waiting for Billy along with Robin. She'd come to their wedding, and she would be pissed at the way Billy was acting. Billy was pissed at himself, but he couldn't seem to think through the panic. He realized that what he was doing was wrong and that it was the worst way to do it, but he couldn't stop, and he couldn't marry Robin. He didn't love him that way, not anymore.

Billy swallowed and tried to ignore the prickle of tears in his eyes. He couldn't think about Robin right now. He had to think about himself and what he was doing, even though it was the stupidest thing he'd ever done in his life.

Billy's phone started vibrating in its spot in the passenger seat. He should have turned it off, and the fact that he hadn't pointed to how scared he'd been. He didn't even know *why* he'd been scared. If he'd talked to Robin, Robin would have understood. He would have been hurt and angry, but then, he would be in this situation, too. This was even worse, because he would also feel betrayed, and he would be right.

Billy waited until his phone stopped vibrating to snatch it from the seat. He didn't even look at who had been calling. He turned it off and threw it back onto the seat when he was done. He tried to swallow around the knot in his throat, but it wasn't easy. Nothing in this situation was easy.

And Billy was to blame.

Instead of waiting until their wedding day, he should have talked to Robin a long time ago. Billy should have explained that while he loved Robin, he wasn't in love with him, and he didn't want to marry him. He liked being with Robin, though, and he'd thought he could do this. Robin was familiar and warm, and it had been easy to go along with this. They'd been together a long time, and marriage was the next step for them.

Or at least, it would have been if Billy hadn't freaked out.

He eyed his phone. Robin, Billy's mother, and his best friend were undoubtedly calling and trying to get through to him. They would be worried that something had happened to him, which made him feel even guiltier. He had to let them know he was fine, but he would have to turn his phone on again. He couldn't do that while driving, which meant he would have to stop.

He pulled over at the next gas station. His hands trembled when he took the phone and turned it on. As soon as it powered up, texts and missed calls started arriving. Billy ignored all of them, quickly texted his best friend that he was okay, then turned the phone off again. Jude would tell both Billy's mother and Robin about the text, and they would be reassured, at least for a while. They would want answers, and Billy would have to give those to them. He didn't know how he would do that, and he didn't want to think about it right now. Right now, the only thing he wanted to think about was going home to his mother's apartment in Green Hill, the place where he'd grown up. He'd never thought he'd want to spend any length of time there again, considering how much he wanted to leave when he was a teenager, yet here he was.

Once the phone was off, Billy left the gas station, headed to Green Hill. Hopefully, his mother wouldn't mind when she came back to find him in her apartment. She would be angry, and she would make sure Billy knew that, and Billy wasn't planning on protesting. Everyone would be mad at him, and it would be their right to decide they never wanted to see him again. Right now, he wished *he* never had to see himself again.

He'd made a mess of his life, and he had no idea how to fix it, or even if he could. Robin wouldn't want to talk to Billy again, and Billy wouldn't blame him.

He drove through lunchtime, not caring if he didn't eat. He wasn't hungry anyway. Right now, he and Robin were supposed to be having their first meal as a married couple. Robin had planned everything, and Billy knew that they'd been supposed to have their first dance after the meal. All their friends had been invited, and now, all of them would be witnesses to Robin's pain and Billy's bad decisions. Billy had no doubt he'd lost them, except hopefully his mother and Jude. If he lost them, too, he didn't know what he would do, although he supposed he would find out sooner rather than later.

He almost cried when he finally drove into Green Hill. The town was still small, but he couldn't help but notice that things had changed since the last time he'd been here. How long had it been? Four, maybe five years? Jude had loved coming to visit Billy's mother, but Billy had avoided it any time he could. He'd thought that coming back would be a defeat, yet he hadn't been able to think about any other place he would feel safe when he'd run.

He turned the car onto Main Street. A few of the shops he'd frequented when he'd been a kid and a teenager weren't there anymore, replaced by shinier, more popular shops. He frowned when he saw that the candy shop was gone. In its place was a shop that sold handmade soap, from what he could see.

He was so distracted that he only saw the man crossing the street at the last moment. He braked, praying he wasn't about to run over the man and add murder to the list of things he needed to repent for. Luckily, the man heard the car, and he jumped out of the way just in time. Billy's car stopped next to him, and the man turned angry eyes to Billy.

"What the fuck?" he yelled. He slammed his hand against the side of Billy's car, making it shake.

Billy was the one who was wrong in this situation, but the man's reaction made his hackles rise. "It was an accident," he yelled through the window.

The man flipped him the bird. "Fuck that, and fuck you. If you can't drive, leave the car at home."

Billy resisted the urge to tell the man to fuck off. It would make everything worse, and he couldn't deal with that right now. His life was already a disaster as it was. There was no need for him to add to it.

Niall watched the car drive down Main Street. He was pissed, and he kind of wanted to go after the guy who'd been driving and make sure he understood just how dangerous what he'd done had been. If Niall hadn't been careful, he would have ended up under that car, and he could think of nothing worse right now. He had to focus on his father and his siblings and not add to the situation. That guy had almost flattened him, and if Niall hadn't noticed the car, he would have.

"Niall? Everything okay?" Val asked.

Niall shook himself. "I'm fine. He didn't hurt me."

Val patted Niall's shoulder. "Good. Simon is waiting."

Niall sighed. He and Val were meeting Simon after work—even though Val had already seen him after lunch—and he wasn't sure it was a good idea. He had no clue what he was supposed to say to Simon. They weren't friends, and they never would be if Niall didn't give Simon a chance. Simon wasn't going anywhere, not when he and Val had already bonded. Niall needed to get used to him, and for Val, they had to become at least friendly. Val deserved it, and Niall never wanted to hurt his best friend.

"I know you don't like him," Val said as they walked toward the bar.

Niall thought about denying it, but he was pretty sure Val could see right through his lies. "It's not that I don't like him," he said.

"It's that you don't know if you can trust him."

"I don't know him, but I'm sure that he's a good guy. He has to be, if he's your mate."

Val arched a brow. "If?"

"You know what I mean. You would never end up mated to someone who doesn't deserve you. I'm just not sure what to make of him. I never thought you would end up bonded to a shifter, and we know next to nothing about the pride, even though they've been there for decades."

"I already told you why that was."

"I know, and I promise I'll give Simon a chance. It's just weird to think of you bonded to him." And maybe Niall was a bit jealous. He didn't want a mate, but he wouldn't reject having a boyfriend. Now that Val was spending a lot of time with Simon, Niall found himself alone most of the time. He didn't begrudge Val or Simon for that, but it had made him realize that he was over one-night stands and short relationships.

His phone vibrated in his pocket, and he took it out, grinning when he saw it was his sister. "Shona is calling."

"Have you talked to her and Flynn?"

"Not yet. I don't want to do it over the phone, and it would be easier to talk to both of them at once. I texted them and told them we need to talk, but that's it." He answered the call. "Hey."

"Where are you?"

Niall sniffed. "Not even a *hello*? Not an *I miss you*?"

Shona snorted. "All of that. Where are you?"

"In town. Why? Do you need anything?"

"Flynn is coming over for dinner. Since you wanted to talk to both of us, I thought it might be a good idea to invite you, too."

"I have something to do with Val and his mate."

Val grabbed Niall's shoulder and squeezed to get his attention. When Niall looked at him, he shook his head and murmured, "Go. Simon and I will be here when you're done, and you need to talk to your sister."

Niall was dismayed that he wouldn't get to spend the evening with his best friend but also relieved that he wouldn't have to spend the evening trying to find something to say to Simon. "Thank you," he told Val before turning his attention back to the phone call. "I'll be right there. I can see Val later or tomorrow."

"Are you sure?" Shona asked.

"Give me fifteen minutes, and I'll be at your place."

"Good. I'm curious about what you wanted to talk about."

Niall hadn't wanted to scare his brother and his sister. He'd also started to wonder if maybe he was imagining things, but he was sure he wasn't. Their father was hiding something, and he needed to find out what it was.

He hung up and turned to Val. "I'm sorry."

"Don't worry about it and go. Let me know if they noticed anything. I want to be involved."

"I'll text you if anything happens. Have fun with Simon, and apologize to him for me."

"He'll understand."

Niall hoped he would. Even though he didn't know how to deal with Simon, he would have to learn to.

He got to Shona's apartment in just under fifteen minutes. He could smell her cooking from outside the door, and it made his stomach grumble. He could do with a homemade meal. At thirty-seven, he should probably be able to cook for himself, but he was useless in the kitchen. He survived on takeout, and he wasn't ashamed of it. Most people wouldn't know where to start if they had to renovate a house, but he did. On the other hand, he had no idea where to start in the kitchen.

He knocked, and his brother opened. Flynn grinned when he saw Niall, then punched Niall's shoulder. "I was starting to wonder if you were dead and no one had noticed."

"Val would notice," Niall pointed out as he walked into the apartment.

"But he's the only one you see regularly. You do know he's not related to you, right?"

"I would see you more often if you weren't so annoying."

Flynn tried to punch Niall again, but Niall sidestepped him. Flynn huffed and followed Niall toward the kitchen, where Shona was doing something at the stove. Niall's stomach growled even louder, so loud that she heard him and turned around, laughing. "It's almost ready. Why don't the two of you set the table and sit down?"

They obeyed, moving around the kitchen and Shona. They were used to this because they tried to have dinner together at least once a month, but it had been two months because they'd been too busy. Niall realized he'd missed his siblings, and he promised himself to try harder to see them, even if it wasn't both at once.

Once they were sitting around the table, Shona pointed her fork at him. "Start talking."

Niall had hoped he could wait until they were done eating, but he'd been the one to tell Shona and Flynn they needed to talk about something, and it was normal that they were curious. He swallowed the bite of food he'd been eating and cleaned his mouth. "It's about Dad. I think he's hiding something."

"Hiding what?" Flynn asked.

"I don't know. I went to his house a few weeks ago, and he wouldn't let me in."

Flynn's eyebrows rose high on his forehead. "Why?"

"He said he was cleaning and that the floor was wet, but I know something was up. He was only wearing sweatpants."

"I agree that something is going on," Shona said. "I called him the other day, but he didn't have time to talk. When I asked him what was going on, he said he was watching a movie, but I'm sure I heard someone there."

"It could have been the movie," Flynn pointed out.

"It didn't sound like the TV, but maybe you're right. Still, I agree with Niall. Dad is hiding something. I want to know what it is."

"It's his business."

"What if he's sick?" Niall asked. He didn't want to burden his siblings with those thoughts, but he also didn't want to be the only one to have them. Maybe Flynn or Shona knew something he didn't.

"Why do you think he's sick?" Shona asked.

Niall shrugged. "I don't know. What else could he be hiding from us?"

"We won't lose him."

"I hope not. I'm worried, though. I don't know what else he could be hiding. If he's sick, it would make sense that he doesn't want us to know after what happened with Mom."

"He wouldn't hide something like that from us," Flynn said. He sounded convinced, and Niall hoped he was right.

"Maybe not, but do you want to risk it? I think we need to confront him and ask him outright what's going on. Whatever it is, we can help him with it, but only if he tells us."

"What if it doesn't have anything to do with his health?"

"I hope it doesn't." But just in case, he needed to know. He'd already lost one parent, and he knew that eventually, he would lose his father, too. He wasn't ready for that, and he would do whatever he could to make sure his dad was okay. The only way for him to do that was to know what was going on.

Billy's bedroom hadn't changed. He'd expected his mother to turn it into something else, maybe a home gym or a room for her crafts, but instead, when he walked in, it was like going back to his teenage years. His posters were still there, and the comforter was the same. Billy would have known about it if he and Robin had stayed with his mom when they'd visited, but he'd felt uncomfortable, and Robin had agreed the best thing to do was to stay at a bed and breakfast.

Billy supposed they wouldn't have to worry about that anymore. Robin wasn't going to visit again, and the thought made a pang of guilt tear through Billy.

He was an asshole. He should have talked to Robin instead of running, but while he knew he'd done the wrong thing, he couldn't seem to be able to fix it, not right now. Even though he was home, panic still swelled in his chest at the thought of marrying Robin and spending the rest of his life with him.

Billy toed off his shoes and climbed under the comforter, wrapping it around his shoulders and holding on tight.

Why was the thought of spending the rest of his life with Robin so terrifying? He loved Robin, even though he wasn't in love with him. They'd been good together, and he knew that Robin loved him. He wouldn't have wanted to marry him if he hadn't. Billy had enjoyed the life they'd had together, and he knew he could have continued. But Robin would have wanted children, and Billy would have found himself entwined even more into a life he wasn't satisfied with. Now that he gave himself time to think about it, he realized that was what had happened.

He'd been okay with Robin. He was used to it, and he couldn't imagine his life without Robin in it. Marrying him had been one step too many, though. The thought of doing it had made Billy understand that he didn't want his life to be what it had been until now. He loved Robin, but he wanted to be *in* love with the person he would eventually marry. He wanted to *want* to marry them, not to panic at the thought.

He was going to have to make amends, and he didn't know where to start or how to do it. There was no way around it, though. He'd made a huge mistake, and he would have to find a way to fix it. He'd never meant to hurt Robin, but he had, and it made him feel even worse than the marriage debacle did.

Billy wasn't sure how long he stayed there, bundled up in his childhood bed, thinking about Robin and the life they could have had together. The sky outside the window turned dark, and still, Billy didn't move. He wasn't hungry, and he wasn't ready to face the world, whatever was waiting for him. He didn't move even when he heard a key in the front door lock and the door open. The only person who had a key other than him was his mother, and she was home.

Billy listened to her footsteps. She closed the door, then came straight to his bedroom. The door flung open, and the light turned on. Billy screwed his eyes shut and pulled the comforter higher on his head, but a second later, it was pulled away from him. He blinked and sat up, looking at his mother, who was holding the comforter against her chest and glaring at him.

"What were you thinking?" she asked.

"I'm sorry I made you worry."

She looked like she wanted to hit him, but she never had, and he knew she wouldn't start now. Instead, she pointed her index finger at him. "You didn't want me to worry? Are you *serious*? You disappeared moments before your wedding, and you only texted Jude to let us know you were okay. I didn't even know where you were or if something had happened to you."

"I said I was okay."

She threw the comforter into Billy's lap. "You weren't okay, Billy. If you had been, you would have been there and marrying Robin. What happened? Why are you here? Why aren't you with Robin, wearing his ring? Do you know what you did to him?"

Billy's eyes prickled again, and this time, he didn't try to stop the tears from rolling down his cheeks. He raised a hand to wipe them away, but others were already coming down, and a few seconds later, he found himself sobbing. "I never meant to hurt him," he said between two sobs.

He couldn't see well because of the tears, but his mother crouched in front of him. She took his hand, and he was so relieved that she wasn't pushing him away that he threw himself into her arms. She made a startled sound, but she wrapped her arms around him and allowed him to cry.

It was like when he was a child. She smoothed down his hair, rubbed his back, and murmured that everything would be okay in his ear. He knew it wouldn't be, but for one moment, he allowed himself to believe his mother.

"What's going on?" she asked once the tears had dried up.

The thought of telling her what he'd done made Billy want to cry again. Instead, he swallowed and looked at the floor. "I panicked. I never wanted to hurt Robin, but the thought of marrying him freaked me out. I left the apartment to go to the ceremony, but instead, I came here."

"What made you panic that way?"

"I don't love him, and when I thought about a life with him, I knew I couldn't do it."

"And you decided to run instead? Oh, Billy. Why didn't you tell him?"

"I didn't want to hurt him."

"What do you think you did? You didn't just hurt him. You made him look like a fool. If the two of you had broken up privately, it would have been easier on him. Instead, he stood there waiting for you while everyone wondered where you were. He kept hope, even after half an hour. I watched him crumble with my own eyes, and I hate that you did that to him. He didn't deserve it."

Billy rubbed his eyes. "I know. He never deserved to be hurt. I shouldn't have done this, and I wish I could take it back."

"But you can't. What are you going to do to make amends?"

"I don't know. I have to call him and apologize, but I'm not sure he'll take my calls."

"I wouldn't, if I were him." Billy's mom sighed. "Although I suppose he'll be glad to know you're okay. He was worried something had happened to you and that you had an accident or something like that. Jude told him you texted that you were okay but not coming, and he was destroyed. He didn't understand how you could do that to him, and honestly, I don't either. I'm glad you're okay, and really, it's all that matters, but I don't understand."

Billy shook his head. He was pretty sure Robin would be dismayed that nothing happened to him. Right now, he probably wished that Billy was dead or something like that. "I don't understand it, either. I really thought I was going to marry him when I got into the car. I was thinking about it. Robin and I have been together for so long."

Billy's mom looked at him. "Maybe that's the problem. You said you don't love him, yet you stayed with him. Why?"

"I don't know. I mean, I do love him, even though I'm not in love with him. I never wanted to hurt him, and I let things go too far. I wanted to be in love with him and to give him everything he ever wanted in life."

"Instead, you humiliated him. I don't know if he'll ever be able to forgive you."

"I don't know if I'll ever be able to forgive myself." But that didn't matter. Billy had done the worst thing he could do to Robin, and he was going to have to find a way to fix it. He didn't know if he could.

His mom got to her feet. "You can stay here for as long as you need. I won't kick you out."

"Thank you. I'm pretty sure I'm going to be moving back to Green Hill, at least for now."

"That's fine. You won't be able to avoid Robin forever, though. He deserves an explanation, and you should probably get your things from the apartment." She hesitated. "You can stay here, but I'm not going to change my life just because you live with me now. I expect you to accept that."

Billy had no idea what she was talking about, but he nodded. "I'm not planning on ruining your life the way I ruined Robin's."

She patted Billy's shoulder. "I know it feels like it, but you didn't ruin Robin's life. You might not have done the right thing, but it would have been worse if you'd waited until after you two were married. Robin will understand that, in time. Don't expect him to forgive you anytime soon, though."

"I don't." How could Robin forgive Billy when even Billy couldn't forgive himself?

CHAPTER TWO

Niall bounced his knee as he waited for Flynn and Shona in his truck. Last night over dinner, they'd agreed to confront their father. The sooner they did it, the better Niall would feel, which was why they'd decided to do it today. He was the first to arrive because he'd left work early. He'd been unable to focus, and the best thing to do was to head out before he got hurt. The problem was that now he was waiting, and it was making him even more nervous.

A knock on the driver's side window made him jump, and he glared at his brother. Flynn raised his hands and shrugged while Niall got out of the truck.

"Didn't mean to scare you," Flynn said.

"You just startled me."

Flynn stared until Niall was uncomfortable. "You're taking this really hard," Flynn commented.

"What I don't understand is why you're not."

"I'm not convinced Dad has health problems."

"But you do agree he's hiding something."

"I do, but he's an adult. It could be anything, and since he's not telling us, I think it's his business."

Niall crossed his arms over his chest. "Why are you here, then?"

"Because you and Shona wanted to come, and I wanted to support you. Besides, it might be Dad's business, but I'm curious. If he tells you what's going on, I want to hear it, too."

"But you don't think it's bad."

"I don't understand why you jumped to that conclusion.

20

It's not like Mom hid the fact that she had breast cancer."

She hadn't. She'd told her children as soon as she'd found out, and they'd lived with it until she died. The thing Niall was afraid of was losing his father as well as losing his mother. He wouldn't be able to deal with it, and he hoped that wasn't the case. "Whatever it is, I want to know."

"Even if it's not health-related?"

Flynn's words made Niall feel slightly guilty. He didn't want his father to feel like he was forced to admit to whatever he was hiding, especially if it wasn't bad. Niall knew himself, though. He wouldn't be able to stop thinking about this until he knew what was going on. "I'm not sure I would be able to believe him if he tells us it's not health-related but doesn't explain it," Niall admitted. "I don't like this, and I wish I didn't have to do it, but I hope Dad will understand."

Thankfully, the conversation was broken by Shona's arrival. She parked behind Niall's truck and got out, grabbing her purse before she closed the door of her car and headed toward Niall and Flynn. "Ready?"

She looked excited, and Niall didn't understand it. Why did neither of his siblings see how bad this could turn? Although maybe that wasn't a bad thing. Niall was the eldest, and he should be the one carrying the weight in the family. If their father had health problems, he would make sure to help him and that his siblings were okay dealing with it.

"As ready as we can be," Flynn answered.

Together, they walked toward the house. The three of them had grown up here, and while Niall had been afraid his father would sell the house after their mother died, he hadn't. He still lived there, and he hadn't given any indication that he wanted to leave. It soothed something in Niall to know that his family home would always be there. Of course, things might change if their father had health problems, but Niall didn't want to think about that just yet.

Niall took the lead, knocking on the door. They waited for their father to open, and when he did, his eyes went wide. "What are the three of you doing here?"

"We want to talk to you," Niall answered.

His father looked wary, but he stepped aside to let them in. Flynn was the last one to walk into the house, and he closed the door behind himself. Niall looked around, but nothing was amiss.

"What's going on?" their father asked.

"We want to know the same," Niall answered.

Shona gently touched Niall's arm. "Maybe this isn't the best way to do this," she murmured before turning her attention to their father. "We're worried about you. Niall and I agree that you're hiding something, and he's afraid it's health-related. That's why we're here. You don't have to tell us if you don't want to, but if you have health problems, we'd like to know and to help you out."

He blinked. "What makes you think I have health problems?"

"Nothing specific. We just want to be sure it's not that."

He rubbed the back of his neck and looked around.

Niall was now more than ever convinced he was hiding something. "Just tell us," he begged.

His father sighed. "Fine. I'll tell you, even though it's none of your business, and I was planning to tell you anyway once it was more serious."

The bottom of Niall's stomach dropped. "You're sick, aren't you?"

His father shook his head. "I'm not. I'm dating someone."

Niall wondered if he'd heard that right. "I'm sorry?"

"I'm dating someone. A woman."

"That's wonderful," Shona said.

She let go of Niall to go to their father, leaving Niall standing there not knowing how to react to that. He hadn't expected his father to be dating, although maybe he should have. It had been ten years since his mother had died, and his father was still young. Of course he would want someone else in his life, even though he'd loved Niall's mother very much. He'd been as destroyed by her death as Niall and his siblings had, which probably explained why he'd waited ten years before doing this.

"Tell us about her," Shona said. She took their dad's arm and dragged him toward the living room.

Niall couldn't do anything but follow. He had no idea what to think, but his siblings were taking it well, and Niall should probably follow their example. He *was* happy for his father, even though he wanted to know more about the woman he was dating.

"Her name is Maris," his father said. "She's a goat shifter."

That stopped Niall in his tracks. "You're dating a shifter?"

Shona glared at Niall, but he ignored her. What was happening? First, his best friend dated a shifter, now his father. Were Shona and Flynn going to start dating shifters, too?

His father crossed his arms over his chest. "Do you have a problem with that?"

"What about her mate? What will happen if she finds him?" He didn't want his father to get his heart broken.

"He died. You don't have to worry about that. Or were you worried because she's a shifter?"

Niall didn't know how to answer that. He was worried because she was a shifter, but saying it out loud would make him sound like an asshole, which he probably was. "I don't care what she is. I just don't want you to get hurt."

His father's expression softened. "I understand that, but you shouldn't be. I'm the father, not you. I know what I'm doing, and I'm not going to stop. Maris is perfect for me, and I think I'm pretty much perfect for her."

"And we're happy for you," Shona said. She was still

glaring at Niall, silently daring him to continue pushing the issue.

Niall wanted to, but he knew better. His sister was going to kick his ass as soon as they were out the door, whether or not he kept his mouth shut. "Is she part of the pride?" he asked his father.

"She never was part of any shifter group. She's lived here all her life with her son, although he's not in town anymore. She lost her mate when she was young, before meeting his father. And I'm happy, Niall. I never thought this would happen to me again, and while I was cautious in the beginning, I don't want to be anymore. She's good for me, and I don't want to break up with her, even if it's for your sake. You're not a child anymore, and you don't have a say in my life."

"I'm allowed to be worried."

"You are, although I'm sorry you feel that way. I promise that Maris is a good person. We've been taking things slow, which is why I haven't told you yet, but maybe it was time. I can see this being serious, so much that I'm thinking about asking her to move in with me eventually. And I'm not forgetting your mother."

Niall groaned. "I didn't even mention Mom. We all know you loved her, but she's been gone ten years. I don't think any of us has a problem with you having a girlfriend. We just don't want to see you hurt."

"I won't be, but you'll have to trust me on that."

Niall *was* going to have to, but the fact that Maris was a shifter made him worry. Like his father had said, though, he didn't have a say in his life, no matter what he thought or felt.

When Billy blinked his eyes open, it took him a moment to remember what had happened. He hadn't been able to sleep most of the night, which was why he'd slept most of the day.

Now, the sky outside his window was dark, and he had no idea what time it was. For the first time in two days, he was hungry, and even though he wasn't looking forward to dragging himself out of his bed, he knew he would have to eventually. He might as well do it now, since he could smell that his mother had cooked.

He pushed himself away from the pillow. He was pretty sure his hair was all over the place, but for once, he didn't care. It wasn't like anyone would see him.

He made a pit stop in the bathroom, avoiding looking at his reflection. Right now he hated himself, and seeing his face would make everything worse.

He couldn't help but wonder what Robin was doing. They were supposed to be on their honeymoon, but Billy was in his childhood bedroom instead, and Robin was God knew where. Had he left? Billy had heard about abandoned spouses going on their honeymoon on their own, and he hoped Robin had done that. He deserved a vacation and time to relax, although knowing him, he was probably back at the apartment they'd shared.

It made Billy feel even worse. He still had no idea what had possessed him to run away minutes before his wedding. He'd really thought he was going to go through with it, and he'd been looking forward to the honeymoon. Instead, he'd run away, and he'd made a mess of everything. He would have to find a way to fix it, but he had no idea where to start.

Once he was done in the bathroom, he headed to the kitchen. His mother was waiting for him, sitting at the small breakfast nook with two steaming mugs in front of her. She smiled when she heard Billy walk into the room and gestured at the seat in front of her. "I made tea. Dinner is on the way, but you're going to have to wait a bit longer."

Billy slid into the chair and wrapped his hands around the mug. The warmth felt good, and even though it hurt a bit, he kept his fingers on the mug. He felt like he deserved a bit of pain after what he'd done.

He could tell his mother wanted to talk about what had happened, but that was the last thing he wanted. He'd already told her what he'd done last night, and he didn't want to rehash it. "What's going on in your life?" he asked.

She looked at him like she knew what he was doing, but thankfully, she didn't call him on it. "You really want to know?"

"Of course I do." And her question made him feel guilty about that, too. He should have paid more attention to her in the past, but he hadn't wanted to come back to Green Hill often, and it had been easy to allow his life to distract him.

She stared at him for a moment longer before nodding. "All right. I suppose everything is the same way it's always been. I go to work, go to the grocery store, things like that."

"That's not what I was asking. I know you do all these things. I want to know if there's something new in your life. We haven't talked in too long."

Her cheeks flushed, and she looked away.

Billy sat up straighter. "There *is* something, isn't there?" he asked.

She huffed but smiled. "There is. I wasn't sure I should tell you now, because it's recent, but since you're asking, I'm dating someone."

Billy blinked. That was the last thing he'd expected. As far as he could remember, his mom had never dated. Maybe she had, and she hadn't told him, but that meant she'd never been serious about any of the men she'd gone out with. This time she was, because she wouldn't be telling Billy about it otherwise.

Billy knew his mother had met and lost her mate when she was younger. They'd been teenagers, and they'd been planning on getting bonded as soon as they were old enough.

He'd died, though, and she'd been destroyed. Then, the next man she'd allowed into her life had gotten her pregnant before leaving her. That was Billy's father, and he hoped he would never have to meet the asshole. As far as Billy knew, she hadn't dated anyone since then. He was twenty-nine now, so it had been a long time.

"It's serious?" he asked.

"I think it could be. I *want* it to be. That's the only reason I'm telling you."

"You wouldn't if you didn't want this to work. What's his name?"

"Regan. He lost his wife ten years ago to breast cancer, and he told me he hasn't dated anyone since then."

"But you changed that."

Her cheeks turned even redder. "I didn't mean to. We started talking at the park one day, and it was nice. The next time I went, he was there again, and we continued seeing each other that way for a while."

"Did you ask him out, or did he?"

"He did. It was obvious he was hesitant, but I wasn't going to say no. He has three children, you know, and he wasn't sure how they'd take it. I hope the four of you will be friends."

Billy leaned back into his chair. So his mother truly hoped it would be permanent. He didn't have a problem with it. He wanted his mom to be happy, and if that happiness came through Regan, he would welcome the man. "I can't make any promises, but I'd like to meet him."

His mom beamed. "Good. I was going to wait to tell you about him because of the wedding and because I'm still not sure how this will turn out, but now you're here, and you're going to notice something is going on."

"You don't have to give me explanations, Mom. You're an adult, and this is your home. I'm not going to ask you not to have him spend the night or anything like that."

If her cheeks turned any redder, they'd explode. "He's not going to spend the night. I usually stay at his house."

Billy arched a brow. "I see. Well, feel free to continue living your life as if I weren't here. I don't want you to change anything just because I'm an asshole."

Her expression shifted. "Have you talked to Robin yet?"

Billy tightened his hands around his mug. "I just woke up, so no."

"You should call him."

She was right. That didn't mean Billy was going to do it. "To tell him what?"

"How about that you're sorry for a start?"

"I *am* sorry. I wish I could take all of this back and not hurt him, but I can't. I wouldn't be surprised if he didn't want to talk to me."

"He might not, but that's his decision to make, not yours. You need to call him and explain what happened. If he doesn't answer, text him, or email him. Tell him how you feel and why you did what you did. That's all you can do in this situation, and even though it's not going to fix things, it's a step forward."

She got up to check on whatever she was cooking in the oven, but Billy stayed where he was, staring at the tea in his mug. He *should* call Robin and apologize, but the thought was petrifying. It was as if every time Billy thought he was ready, he really wasn't, and his body and his mind stopped him from doing the right thing.

It was a stupid explanation, but he couldn't change the panic that gripped his gut when he thought about explaining to Robin what had happened. He would do it, eventually.

But not now.

Niall continued thinking about what his father had said as he headed toward the bar. He'd called Val so they could have an emergency beer, and he couldn't wait to get there and complain to his best friend.

He wasn't even sure what he had to complain about. He wasn't the one dating Maris, after all. He also wasn't the one dating Simon, so he really didn't have a say in any of this. That didn't change the fact that he was worried, mostly for his father, but also for Val. At least Simon was Val's mate and they were bonded, which meant Simon wasn't going to abandon him. The same couldn't be said for Maris, although her mate's death made Niall feel better. That made him feel like an asshole, but he was looking out for his father, not for her.

All in all, he didn't know what to think about what had just happened, which hopefully would change once he talked to Val.

He was the first to arrive at the bar, and he chose a table in the back so he and Val could talk. He ordered a beer along with fries and onion rings, just to eat something, since he hadn't had dinner. He didn't really feel up to eating, but he knew better than to drink on an empty stomach.

By the time Val arrived, Niall had demolished all the food and was on his second beer. He was grateful he was done eating when he saw that Simon was behind Val. It took everything Niall had not to groan. Instead, he smiled at Simon and got to his feet. "I didn't expect you to come along."

"I wasn't going to, but Val insisted. He said you wouldn't mind."

Niall looked at Val, who was glaring at him as if to tell him that he better not mind, or else. Niall plastered a smile on his face and turned his attention back to Simon. "Of course not. Sit down. I already started without you, but I was starving."

"Don't worry about us. We already had dinner." Simon turned to Val. "Do you want me to get you something?"

"I can grab us a beer."

"Sit down with Niall. I'll go."

"You're sure?"

"I wouldn't be offering if I wasn't." Simon kissed the top of Val's head. "Relax. I'll be right back."

Niall couldn't look away. It was evident that both Simon and Val were happy. Niall might be wary of Simon, but he didn't really have a good reason. Simon was perfect for Val, and there was no denying that.

Val watched Simon thread his way toward the bar for a moment before turning to Niall. "All right. What's going on?"

Niall swallowed. "Nothing."

"We both know that's bullshit. Is it Simon? I know I didn't tell you he was coming, but I didn't expect to see you tonight. I wasn't going to spend another evening away from him."

Niall shook his head. "I already said I have nothing against his presence here."

"And I don't believe that. What's your problem with him?"

"I don't have a problem with him. I'm just not sure what to think of the pride. They're weird, and it's strange that we didn't know about Simon before you met him. I'm just worried about you getting hurt, I promise."

Val's expression softened. "I understand that, and I'm grateful, but you don't have to be worried. Simon isn't going to hurt me. I'm also not going to hurt Simon. We're mates, and we're making things work. Is that truly the only problem you have?"

"What else should be happening?"

Val shrugged a shoulder. "I don't know. Simon asked if you were jealous."

Niall had been taking a sip of his beer, and he almost choked himself as he swallowed. "Why would I be jealous?"

"You tell me."

"I'm not jealous. You're my best friend, and I've never looked at you differently. If Simon is worried about that, you can reassure him. I'm not going to try to steal you away from him."

"Good, because I wouldn't come. No offense, but I only see you as a friend, too."

"I wouldn't know what to do if you didn't."

"What's going on, then? Why did you ask me to come over tonight?"

Now that Val and Simon were here, Niall realized how stupid he'd been. Of course his best friend had plans with his mate. Their conversation could have waited until tomorrow morning. There was nothing Niall could or should do about his father's situation. He'd promised to tell Val what he'd found, and he would, but that was it. It wasn't bad, and it *definitely* could have waited.

He sighed and took another sip of beer. "I talked to my father. Well, we did. Shona and Flynn were there, too."

Val straightened in his chair. "And? What's going on?"

"He's dating someone."

Val's eyes widened. "I never thought I'd hear those words."

"I never thought he'd date again."

"Is that why you're pissed off? Because you don't want him to date?"

Niall shook his head. "I don't care about that. My mom has been gone for ten years, and it's his life. I don't care if he dates."

"But?"

"But he's dating a shifter."

Val waited for a moment, and when Niall didn't add anything, he asked, "Why is that a problem?"

Niall didn't want to offend anyone, least of all Val. "It's not a problem. I'm just not sure what to think of it."

"Are you afraid she'll meet her mate and dump your father?"

"That's not going to happen. Apparently, her mate died a while back. I'm just not sure what to think of this."

"I don't understand what there is to think about. Your father met someone he likes, and he's dating her. That's all there is to it. The fact that she's a shifter doesn't matter." He paused and frowned. "Or at least, it shouldn't."

"It doesn't matter, not really. I'm just worried about him. We don't really know a lot about shifters, not when the pride stayed hidden for so many years."

Val groaned. "We're back to this, then?"

"I'm sorry. I know you don't care about that, and I wish I could, too. I can't help but be worried."

"There's no reason for you to be worried. Shifters are people, just like you and me. It's not going to change her relationship with your father. Besides, it's *their* relationship, not yours. You don't have a say in it, and I hope you won't do something stupid that will antagonize both her and your father."

"I'm not an idiot."

"Sometimes, though, you behave like one. I really don't understand what you have against shifters. Yes, the pride stayed hidden for decades, and we barely know them. What does that have to do with you, though? You've met several pride members, and they're good people. You know why the pride stayed hidden for so long. Why is it still a problem?"

Niall wasn't sure how to explain. "It's not a problem," he said for what felt like the hundredth time. "I just like to know what to expect from people, and I don't when it comes to the pride."

Val huffed. "You don't know what to expect from most people, Niall. Look at your father. Did you expect him to start dating?"

"I didn't."

"See? People will always surprise you, whether or not

they're shifters. I can promise you the pride doesn't want to hurt anyone."

"I'm starting to understand that."

"Even though it's going to take a while for you to accept it. I see, and I kind of understand it, but you have to let go of this. I don't want to have to choose between you and Simon."

"I never would make you choose." Niall was offended that Val expected it, although maybe he shouldn't be. He'd been acting like an asshole, so of course Val would believe that.

"Good. Make sure you don't ask your father to choose, either. Is his girlfriend even part of the pride?"

"He said she isn't. I think he mentioned she was a goat shifter."

"See. You don't have to worry. You don't like the pride, and that's your prerogative, but your father's girlfriend isn't part of the pride. You don't have anything against her." He paused and turned more serious. "You're going to lose your father if you're not careful. From what you're telling me, he's happy for the first time in a while. You're not asking me to choose, but please, make sure you're not asking him, either."

Billy tried to escape to his bedroom as soon as dinner was over, but his mother cut his path before he could reach the hallway, smiling at him. It made his stomach curdle and the food he'd just eaten feel heavy. He hoped he wasn't going to throw up.

"Why don't we sit down in the living room to talk?" his mother suggested.

"What's there to talk about?"

"There's a lot to talk about. I spent the entire conversation before dinner talking about Regan and me. It's time to talk about you and Robin."

"I don't want to talk about Robin and me."

"Well, I don't care. We're going to talk about it, and we're going to do it now. If you don't, you know where the door is."

"You'll kick me out if I don't agree to talk to you?"

She sighed. "I would never kick you out, not unless you did something awful."

"I'm pretty sure that what I did is awful."

"It wasn't great. That doesn't mean it's awful. I'm not Robin, and while I hate what you did, I can see your side of the story, too."

Billy was surprised. He'd half expected his mother to kick his ass out and tell him to apologize to Robin. He wanted to do it, but he didn't know how. He didn't even know if he had the guts to do something like that.

His mother took his wrist and dragged him into the living room. She pushed him onto the couch, and he knew he wouldn't be able to escape. She sat next to him, crossing one of her legs under herself so they could face each other. "Now talk. Are you still freaking out over what happened?"

"Of course I am. I shouldn't have done it."

"We can agree on that. Why did you, then?"

Billy sighed. He'd had the entire night to think about it, but he still didn't have a good answer. "I don't know. I thought I was going to marry Robin when I left the apartment yesterday morning. I was driving to him, and then, I wasn't."

"Are you saying you didn't realize you were driving to Green Hill?"

"I did. I just couldn't turn back." Billy sucked in a breath. "We've already talked about this. Do we really have to do it again?"

His mother arched a brow. "Have you called Robin?"

"You know I haven't. You asked me before dinner, and it hasn't changed."

"Why haven't you called him? He deserves an explanation."

"And I want to give one to him. The problem is that I don't have one. I don't know why I freaked out and why I left the way I did."

"That's a lie. You know exactly why you freaked out. You told me yesterday that while you love Robin, you're not in love with him, and you couldn't spend the rest of your life with him. Is that still the truth?"

"It is." And that *was* why Billy hadn't been able to marry Robin. That didn't change the fact that he should have talked to him instead of running away.

"Then you have to tell him that. I've always liked Robin. I thought he was good for you, and I still think that. Obviously, though, something happened. He doesn't deserve any of this, Billy. You made your choice, and you have to act like an adult and do the right thing. Hiding here and ignoring the world isn't going to change anything or make it better."

"I promise I'll call him and explain."

"When?"

"When I'm ready, Mom. Can't you understand that I'm not?"

She crossed her arms over her chest. "Do you think Robin was ready to be abandoned at the altar?"

"Don't be so dramatic. We weren't getting married in a church."

"That's not the part that matters. The part that matters is that you hurt him, and you're hurting him even more by hiding."

"Look, I know I'm the one who made a mistake here. I'm not saying you're wrong, and I promise I'll call him. I'm not ready to do it, though, and I don't think I can do it until then. I'm freaking out just at the thought of calling him. Do you really think I would be able to explain what happened if he answered his phone? Because I don't, and I'm pretty sure I'd make even more of a mess if I tried."

She stared at him, and Billy wondered if she was going to kick him out after all. He wouldn't blame her. He'd not only done the wrong thing with Robin and hurt one of the people he cared the most about, but he was still doing the wrong thing by not calling Robin and explaining why he'd done what he'd done. No matter how many times she told him he was making his mistake an even bigger one, he couldn't find it in himself to change things, not right now.

She sighed. "Fine. I'll stop bothering you about this, but please, do the right thing. You can't hide here forever, no matter how much you want to, and Robin doesn't deserve any of this. You say you love him, even though you're not in love with him. Act like you do, then. Show him that he's still important to you. Even if he doesn't answer, even if he starts insulting you, tell him. He deserves at least that, and even though for now, he might not feel like talking to you, he's going to be grateful he has an explanation eventually."

She got to her feet after kissed the top of Billy's head. "I love you, and nothing is going to change that. I don't like what you're doing, though. I'm disappointed."

Bill's stomach churned as he watched her leave the living room. He'd never wanted to disappoint anyone, least of all his mother. She'd sacrificed so much for him, and he felt like a dick for the entire situation. He had to do something to fix this.

The problem was that he felt like he couldn't.

With a sigh, he got up from the couch and headed toward his bedroom. He was starting to feel angsty at the thought of spending so much time there. But he'd made his bed, and now, he had to lie in it. He was in this situation because of his own bad decisions, and nothing would change that. If he wanted to start moving forward, he would have to do something, which he wasn't ready for.

He closed the door behind himself and flopped onto the

bed. His cell phone was on the nightstand. He eyed it, wondering if Robin had tried calling him. He hadn't allowed himself to check the messages and emails yet, but he needed to. His boss knew not to expect him, since he was supposed to be on his honeymoon, but what about Jude? He was going to be *so* angry that he might kick Billy's ass, and Billy wouldn't protest too much. He deserved to be kicked to the curb.

Instead of picking up his cell phone and turning it on, he curled on his side and pulled the comforter over his head. Tomorrow, he would do something. Tonight, he would cry over his bad decisions and berate himself for what he'd done. He would try to convince himself that he needed to call Robin, no matter what Robin would say. Even if Robin insulted him, Billy deserved all of it, while Robin deserved an explanation. Giving him one was the first step toward getting out of this mess.

CHAPTER THREE

Niall was wrong. He never liked admitting it, but in this case, he couldn't avoid it anymore. No matter how wary he'd been of Simon, he and Val were perfect for each other and Val was happy. That was all Niall wanted for his best friend, and it was what Simon gave Val.

The fact that Simon was a shifter didn't matter. It hadn't mattered even in the beginning, whatever Niall had thought. He should have gotten his head out of his ass back then, but he supposed now was better than never.

"You're staring," Val said. He sounded amused.

Niall cleared his throat. "I wasn't." He had been.

"What's going on? Is it your father again?"

Niall hooked his hammer into his belt and leaned against the wall. "He's fine. We're having dinner with him and Maris tonight."

Val arched a brow. "*That's* what you're having trouble with?"

"I'm not having trouble with anything."

"Doesn't look like it to me. I'm not sure I can do much, but you know that if you need to talk, I'm ready to listen."

Niall grimaced. "When did we start talking about feelings?"

"Probably when Simon came into my life. So, do you want to talk about it or not?"

Niall didn't, if anything because he didn't want to admit he'd been wrong. Val already knew he was, though, and hopefully, he wouldn't remind Niall of it. "I'll admit I was wrong about Simon," Niall started, unsure how to continue.

Val clutched his chest. "You admit you were wrong? What's happening? Are you sick?"

Niall was tempted to throw his hammer at him, but even though he was pissed, he wasn't angry enough to hurt his best friend. "Very funny."

"I thought so, too. So now, you're still wary of shifters. Does that go for your father's girlfriend, too?"

Niall sighed. "That's what I was thinking about. I can't deny that Simon is perfect for you, not when I've seen the two of you together, but she's different."

"Only because you haven't seen her and your father together yet. I know you're worried, but I doubt your father would have wanted to introduce you to her if he wasn't sure this was the best thing both for him and for his kids. I wish you'd keep a more open mind when it comes to her."

"I'm trying." And Niall truly was. He could admit he'd been wrong about Simon. He also could acknowledge that he was probably wrong about Maris.

His main gripe with Simon was that he was part of the Green Hill pride. Niall still didn't know what to think of the pride, and he didn't like that they been hiding, even though they'd been in Green Hill for decades. Val had explained why they had, though, and Niall was willing to give them a chance.

He didn't have the same excuse when it came to Maris. She wasn't part of the pride, and she'd never been. She'd lived in Green Hill for close to thirty years, from what Niall's father had said, and she wasn't going anywhere. She was part of the town as much as Niall and his family, and eventually, she'd be part of Niall's life. Niall didn't have a problem with his father dating. He just wondered why his father couldn't date a human lady instead of a shifter one.

"Your father will be happy that you're at least trying," Val said. "But I don't think it's enough. I don't understand what you have against Maris, and I doubt he does."

"That's because I don't have a reason to be wary of her."

"Exactly. I'm grateful you can at least see that. I suppose your father might think you're not sure about her because you don't want him to be hurt. Hopefully, you'll get over it. Just like Simon is perfect for me, I'm sure Maris is perfect for your father."

Niall wasn't going to agree or disagree until he met her. "I suppose we'll find out soon enough. Do you want to come to dinner, too? I could use some support."

Val shook his head. "It's a family matter, and I'm not family. I'm sure I'll meet her soon. Besides, you have your siblings."

"They don't agree with me."

"Makes you wonder why, doesn't it?"

There was the urge to throw his hammer at Val again. Instead, Niall glared at him. "I *know* I'm unreasonable. You don't have to point it out again, not when I can't help how I feel."

"You can't help it, no. You *can* help how you react to those feelings, though. You're aware that what you're feeling is wrong, and you know how you should behave. Treat her well, whatever happens. It doesn't matter if you hate her. It's not your place to say anything or to try to change your father's mind."

Once again, Val was right.

Niall chewed on his words for the rest of the day. He had changed his thoughts and behavior when it came to Simon, and he would do it for Maris, too. Because Val was right—it was none of Niall's business, even if he hated her. She was Niall's father's girlfriend, not Niall's, and he didn't have a say in their relationship. He didn't want his father to get hurt, but he couldn't prevent it. If something happened, he would be there for his dad. That was all he could do.

Even though he had no idea what to expect from the dinner, he dressed as neatly as possible. It wasn't exactly that he wanted to impress Maris,, but he did want to make a decent first impression. He doubted she would break up with his father because Niall was wearing a sweater with a hole or something like that, but he didn't want to risk it, so he put on his best shirt, a clean pair of dark jeans, and his boots.

He felt preppy, and he wasn't used to wearing button-down shirts, but he would do, or at least he hoped so. After one last glance in the mirror, he pushed his hair out of his eyes, making a mental note he needed to get it cut, and headed out the door. He wasn't late yet, but he would be if he wasted another five minutes.

When he got to the restaurant his father had chosen, he saw that both his siblings were already there. Flynn and Shona were standing outside, talking, while Shona was smoking. Niall glared at the cigarette when he reached them, and she rolled her eyes at him.

"You're not my father, and if Dad hasn't managed to make me stop, you won't, either."

"I wish you would. It's not good for you."

"I know. Nothing is good for me, though. I just read an article that said that cabbage isn't good for people."

Niall had no idea what to do with that declaration. "I doubt it gives you cancer."

Shona's expression softened, and she threw the cigarette on the ground, stepping on it. "I'm sorry. I swear I'm trying to stop, but I'm stressed."

"We all are. I can help, if you want me to."

"I'll do it on my own. So, are you ready to meet Maris? Flynn and I just did."

"I can't wait."

Shona frowned. "You don't sound excited. Are you still

angry?"

Did everyone think he was an asshole? Probably, and he supposed they wouldn't be wrong. "I'm not angry. I want Dad to be happy, and if Maris makes that happen, that's perfectly fine with me."

"Are you sure? Because you look like you'd rather be anywhere but here."

Niall pulled on his collar. "That's because I don't like to wear shirts."

"Then you shouldn't have. It's not like you need to impress her."

"Don't I?"

"She's here for Dad, not for you." Shona looked Niall up and down. "You clean up well, though, which is great, because Maris's son is here, too."

Niall remembered his father mentioning that she had a son, but he didn't know anything about the guy. "Was that planned?"

"Not as far as I know. He looks like a good guy, though, and Maris said he recently got out of a relationship. He's gay," she added, wagging her eyebrows.

It was Niall's turn to roll his eyes. "I'm not going to fall in love with him just because he's gay. He's probably not my type."

"I disagree, but I suppose you'll find out. Let's go inside."

Niall and Flynn exchanged an amused glance as Shona hooked her arm under Niall's and pulled him inside. Niall saw his father right away. He was sitting at a table, smiling in a way Niall hadn't seen in years. His cheeks were pink, and he was gesturing as he talked. On the other side of the table sat a woman and a man. Their backs were to Niall so he couldn't see them, but when Niall's father noticed them and rose from his chair, the lady turned around.

"Dad. It's great to see you," Niall said. He turned his

attention to Maris and offered her his hand. "And it's a pleasure to meet you, Maris. I'm Niall."

She smiled. She looked kind and gentle, which Niall supposed was what his father needed.

"I'm Maris, as you already know, and it's a pleasure to meet you, too. Your father told me so much about you."

"Only good things, I hope?"

She laughed. "I suppose every parent only wants to say good things about their children." She turned to the man sitting next to her. "This is my son, Billy."

Niall smiled as the man turned, but it only lasted a few seconds. "You," he said through gritted teeth.

The man who had almost run him over with his car glared back at him.

Billy hadn't expected this. When his mother had mentioned that she was having dinner with her boyfriend and his children, he'd decided to go along. He wanted to meet them, too, especially his mom's boyfriend.

"You know each other?" Billy's mom asked.

Billy forced himself to smile. "Not exactly, no." He didn't want to make a scene, so he offered Niall his hand. "Like my mother said, I'm Billy."

Niall looked at Bill's hand as if it might bite him. "And you're a terrible driver."

Billy didn't want to shake Niall's hand anymore. Instead, he wanted to punch him, and he was sorely tempted to do just that. The only reason he didn't was that his mother didn't deserve this. "I apologize for what happened. I was overwhelmed, and I should have been more careful."

"Damn right, you should have."

Niall turned toward his father, dismissing Billy.

Billy almost mentioned how rude Niall had been, but

instead, he pressed his lips together and sat back in his seat. He might not like Niall, but Regan was nice, and Billy could see how much the man cared for his mom. He wouldn't do anything to ruin that, especially not after what had happened in his own life.

"Why don't you sit next to Billy?" Niall's sister said. Her eyes twinkled with mischief, and even though it made Billy want to smile, he did his best not to.

"I'd rather sit next to you," Niall said, but Shona was already settling down between her father and her other brother, Flynn.

Niall glared at her, but thankfully, he moved toward the chair next to Billy's without protesting. As he passed behind Billy, the air moved, pushing his scent toward Billy's nose. Billy's back went ramrod straight as he tried to process what was happening.

It couldn't be. It shouldn't be possible, not after what had just happened with Robin—after what Billy had done. He couldn't be meeting his mate right now, and his mate couldn't be Niall.

"Everything okay?" Billy's mom asked softly.

Billy forced himself to smile at her. "Everything is perfect."

"Are you sure? You look tense." She hesitated. "Is it still Robin? Have you tried calling him again?"

Billy shook his head. He'd told his mom he'd tried calling Robin, even though it was a lie. He had needed to say it because she wouldn't have stopped asking otherwise. He wasn't ready to confront Robin and for Robin to tell him how disappointed he was and how much he hated him. He would have to eventually, but it could wait.

It had to, especially with what was happening right now.

"So, Billy, tell us about you," Shona said.

Billy cleared his throat. "There's not much to say."

"Your mom said you just came out of a relationship."

Billy had hoped Shona had forgotten that. "I did. I was with Robin for years."

"Why did you break up with him?"

"Shona," her father hissed.

Billy waved at him to let him know it was okay. It wasn't, but he wasn't about to explain why. "I still love him, but I wasn't in love with him anymore."

Shona grimaced. "I'm sorry. I know how that goes, but I'm sure you'll find someone else soon." Her gaze slid to Niall.

Billy swallowed. Did she know something? She was human, just like the rest of her family, and she couldn't know that Billy and Niall were mates. It would have been impossible even if she'd been a shifter. The only one who knew was Billy, and he wasn't about to tell anyone.

He was relieved when the waitress arrived and everyone at the table focused on ordering food. He chose the first thing he found on the menu, not caring what he was about to eat. He also stayed out of the conversations that happened around the table once the waitress left. He didn't know what to say. He hadn't expected anyone to ask him about his relationship with Robin, and even though he'd dodged the bullet, he would have to explain sooner or later.

Or maybe he wouldn't. His mother wasn't going anywhere, and Billy suspected Regan's family would be part of his life for a long time, but Billy didn't have to move back to Green Hill. He could go back to the city and his job, even though he wasn't with Robin anymore.

He didn't want to. He wanted to stay home with his mother, away from the city where he and Robin had been happy and where he had betrayed the man he should have married.

Billy's mother elbowed him in his stomach. "Stop being so grumpy."

He resisted the urge to glare at her. "I'm not grumpy."

"Could have fooled me. You're not even smiling anymore. At least try to have a conversation with Regan and his children, please. I want you to get along with them."

"We *are* getting along."

She didn't look convinced. "What was that between you and Niall, then?"

Billy shook his head. He didn't want to have to explain. "Nothing. I promise I'm doing my best."

Since he'd promised his mother he would try, he turned his attention back to Shona and Flynn. There was no way he was going to talk to Niall. He hadn't expected to meet his mate tonight, and he didn't know how to deal with it, not with everything else that happened.

"What about you?" he asked Shona. "Are you in a relationship?"

It was fairly easy to continue the conversation once it had started. Billy made sure to ignore Niall and his mother's glare, focusing on Regan, Shona, and Flynn.

His mom's phone was on the table, which was surprising, because she was one of those people who didn't want phones to be around when they were eating. She snatched it up when it started vibrating, and Billy wondered who it was. He knew he was in trouble when she grinned and handed the phone to him.

"What is this?" He asked.

"It's Jude."

"Why is he calling you?"

"Because he wants to talk to you."

Billy continued staring at the phone without taking it. His mother sighed and answered, and he listened to her and Jude talk.

They were close. Jude and Billy had been best friends for years, and Billy's mom might as well be another mother to Jude. Sometimes it felt like she preferred Jude, although Billy couldn't blame her in this situation.

"He's almost here," she said as she hung up.

Billy gaped at her. "How is that possible?"

"He called me when he still couldn't get through to you. He was worried, and I told him you were okay. It wasn't enough for him. He wants to talk to you, and I told him to come around." She paused. "You didn't call him. Did you at least call Robin like you said?"

"I already told you I tried, but he didn't answer," Billy lied. The words tasted like metal on his tongue.

She didn't look convinced, but she nodded. "All right. Well, Jude's almost here, and I think you should head out to talk to him before he comes in. I wouldn't care if he had dinner with us, but I don't think you want to explain to Regan's children what happened with Robin."

Billy groaned. "You told Regan, though, didn't you?"

"I did. I wanted advice, and he was the best person to give it to me."

"Great. He has to think I'm horrible now."

"He doesn't. I explained what happened, and while I doubt he thinks you're the greatest person in the world, you're my son. He'll accept you, whatever happens."

Billy pushed his chair back and got to his feet. As he moved, his arm brushed against Niall's, and Billy jerked it back as if the contact had burned him. Niall noticed—because of course he did—and glared at Billy.

Billy couldn't deal with this right now. He couldn't even deal with Jude, but at the moment, that was preferable.

Niall had no idea what's Billy's problem was, and he didn't care. As far as he was concerned, Billy was an asshole, and Niall didn't want to get to know him. He also didn't want to know why Billy seemed to hate him.

Mostly.

The fact that Billy was precisely the kind of man Niall usually dated didn't help. He looked tired, much more than anyone should look, but he was also gorgeous. He was taller than Niall by a few inches, and where Niall was muscled because of his job, Billy was slender. Niall couldn't see much of Billy's body since Billy was dressed, but Billy's messy brown hair and his green eyes made Niall want to mess him up. He wanted to find out what Billy would look like stretched out under him, which would no doubt end up being a disaster Niall couldn't afford. The problem was that even Billy's *freckles* were adorable, and it was hard to reconcile that with how bitchy Billy was acting.

They had started on the wrong foot. Niall could admit that, just like he could admit it was partly his fault. Yes, Billy had almost run him over with his car, and Niall had taken it badly, but now they were part of the same family. It was a strange family Niall had never thought he'd have, but he couldn't deny the way his father looked at Maris. He would eat his hammer if they ever broke up.

From what Niall could see, Maris and his father were in this for the long run, which meant that Billy was going to be part of Niall's life for a while. No matter how irritated Niall was, he needed to make friends with Billy, or at the very least to tolerate him. That wasn't going to be easy if Billy kept staring at Niall as though he'd killed his dog, but now that Niall had admitted he was in the wrong when it came to shifters, he wasn't going to be in the wrong in his relationship with Billy, too. Niall wanted this to work for his father, and he would do everything he could to make that happen.

"Is he okay?" Shona asked Maris, looking at the door of the restaurant where Billy had just disappeared.

Maris sighed and took a sip of wine. "He will be, or at least, I hope so. He has a lot going on in his life right now."

"Because of the break-up."

"Yes. It wasn't easy for him, even though he was the one who broke up with Robin. They're still working things out, and I'm not surprised he's grumpy. I wish things had been different, because I wanted him to make a good impression."

Shona's smile was gentle. "We all understand breakups aren't easy. Don't worry too much. I'm sure Billy is a great person."

Niall almost strangled himself as he tried not to snort loudly. His father frowned, and Niall decided he needed a breath of fresh air. He didn't want to talk to his father about why he and Billy were so antagonistic toward each other. He wouldn't know how to answer since he didn't have a clue.

He got to his feet. "I'm going outside for a bit."

"Don't tell me you started smoking like Shona," Niall's father said.

"Never. I just feel a bit too warm. I promise I'll be right back."

Niall realized his father probably believed he wasn't happy with about Maris, but he was wrong. Niall liked Maris, even though he wasn't quite sure about Billy yet. His first instinct was to dislike Billy after what had happened between them, but he was starting to wonder if there was something more to the situation than he'd thought. Maybe Billy hadn't just been a reckless driver. If there was more, Niall wanted to find out.

He didn't know why he was giving Billy the benefit of the doubt or why he wanted to know what was going on in his life so much, but he was unwilling to analyze his feelings at the moment. Instead, he stepped outside. The door swung closed behind him. It didn't stay closed for long, and when Niall turned, he found his brother had followed him.

"What's going on?" Flynn asked.

Niall narrowed his eyes at him when he saw Flynn take a pack of cigarettes out of his pocket. "Don't tell me you started smoking, too."

"I've always smoked. You just didn't know."

"And you're telling me now?"

"I've already heard everything you had to say to Shona. You didn't have to repeat it for me. I know it's bad for my health, and I promise I'm trying to quit, but this isn't the best evening to do that."

"Why not? Are you nervous?"

Flynn shrugged and lit up one of the cigarettes. Niall took a step back, wrinkling his nose at the smoke.

"I was kind of nervous about meeting her," Flynn admitted. "Weren't you?"

"I didn't know what to expect."

"What do you think now that you've met her? I quite like her. I like how happy Dad is with her even more."

He sounded like he was expecting Niall to disagree, but he couldn't. "They look happy together," Niall admitted. "And she seems nice."

"You're still not convinced."

"I don't know her well enough to be convinced. I'm keeping my mind open, though. She makes Dad happy, and that's all that matters. My opinion doesn't."

"I wouldn't say that. Even though I doubt Dad would break up with her just because you don't like her, your opinion matters. He wants us to be happy as much as we want him to be. He doesn't want to fight with us over this."

Niall bristled, even though Flynn was right. Why should he think Niall accepted Maris when Niall had made it obvious he didn't like his father dating a shifter? "I won't fight with Dad, and I won't force him to choose between Maris and me. I'm not that much of an asshole. If he's happy, then he should be with her. That's all I have to say about it."

"I'm surprised. I thought it would take you much longer to accept this."

"It won't. I don't have a reason to be wary of shifters, including Simon and Maris. I understand that now, and I'll keep that opinion to myself if I ever feel that way again."

Flynn shook his head. "I don't get it. What did shifters do to you? Or is it because you feel like they're taking away people you love? First Val, now Dad. It would make sense."

Niall hadn't thought about that, but maybe he should have. Until Val had met Simon, he and Niall had been thick as thieves. Even though they'd each had relationships in the past, they'd been short and passing. Their friendship hadn't been, and it still wasn't. It was true that Val was spending less time with Niall, though, which Niall supposed had influenced what he thought of Simon.

"I know they're not taking away anyone," he answered cautiously. He didn't want to lie to his brother, but he also needed time to think about this.

"In a way, they are. You've been spending less time with Val, and the same will go for Dad. There's also the fact that Maris will probably move into the house Mom lived in when she was alive. How do you feel about that?"

A movement caught Niall's attention, and he was grateful for the distraction. He had no idea how to answer his brother's questions, and he didn't like feeling like Flynn was psychoanalyzing him. He turned to see Billy waiting in the parking lot, leaning against a car. "What do you think he's doing there?" he asked.

Flynn looked at Billy, too. "I have no idea. Do you actually care? It didn't look like you and Billy were getting along earlier."

"It's none of my business, and I don't care. I was just curious." And he was, but at least to himself, he couldn't deny he did want to know what Billy was doing there, and more importantly, whether he was okay.

Billy shifted from one foot to the other. He wondered what was about to happen.

Jude had to be angry, probably angrier than he'd ever been at Billy. Billy couldn't blame him, but he didn't understand why Jude wanted to talk to him so badly. Surely Billy's mother had explained what had happened?

Billy should have tried talking to Jude before freaking out and leaving, but he hadn't been thinking. He'd been acting on instinct, and if he hadn't, he would have taken time to make decisions, and he wouldn't have run away from Robin the way he had. All of that was in the past, though, and he couldn't change it. Having Jude yell at him wouldn't, either. Billy wasn't looking forward to seeing his best friend, which had to be a first in his life.

He waited, aware of the fact that Niall and his brother were close by looking at him. He'd noticed them when they'd first come out of the restaurant, and he hadn't known what to think about their presence. He half expected Niall to tell him to leave after he'd almost run him over with his car, but thankfully, Niall and Flynn stayed at a distance. They were talking while Flynn was smoking, and Billy did his best to ignore them.

It was hard. How could he ignore the fact that Niall was his mate? He hadn't even begun to wrap his mind around that, and it added to the long list of the problems he had to deal with. The easiest thing was to ignore it, at least for now, and hope it would be enough.

A car turned into the parking lot. Billy tensed then swallowed as he tried to peek through the windshield and recognize the driver. Sure enough, the car parked right next to his mom's, and when Jude stepped out, he looked ready to kill Billy.

"What the fuck were you thinking?" he yelled.

Billy looked around. He didn't want to make a scene, but he knew better than to try to stop Jude. He wouldn't hear reason until he was done saying what he needed to say. "I wasn't thinking," Billy confessed.

Jude strode toward him, leaving his car door open. "Damn right, you weren't. If you'd been thinking, I hope you wouldn't have abandoned Robin the way you did. I hope you wouldn't have disappeared without a word."

"I told you I was okay. I texted you."

Jude had finally reached Billy, and he pushed Billy with both his hands. Luckily, Billy was standing by his mother's car, so he didn't tumble down to the ground. It was close, though.

"You think a text was enough? I was freaking out. Your mother and Robin were freaking out. We thought something had happened to you, that you'd had an accident or something. How could you do this?"

Billy rubbed his face. Once again, he could feel tears prickling his eyes. He'd cried in front of Jude more often than he'd cried in front of anyone else, including Robin, so Jude wouldn't care. He might even try to comfort him if he could get over his anger, something Billy wasn't sure was possible.

"I freaked out," he said. He didn't want to go over this again, but he had to. "I didn't know what I was going to do until I actually did it. I left the apartment to join you and everyone else and marry Robin, but instead, I drove to Green Hill."

"Why?" Jude asked.

Billy shook his head, unable to answer. His throat was tight.

Jude sighed and stepped closer. Billy was tempted to move away in case Jude tried to hit him, but he would deserve it, so he stayed where he was. When Jude reached for him, he winced, and Jude tsked.

"Do you really think I would hit you?" Jude asked as he wrapped his arms around Billy.

Billy could have cried in relief, and he almost did. Instead, he hugged Jude back, taking comfort in the familiar sensations. "I wouldn't have blamed you if you had. I deserve it."

"You do. You deserve so much more than a punch. I can't believe you did this and didn't tell me about it."

"I should have. I know you would have told me not to do it, and you would have been right. I really thought I was ready to marry him, though."

Jude stepped away. Billy wanted him to come back, but he didn't ask, looking around instead. Thankfully, Niall and Flynn were nowhere to be seen. They were no doubt back in the restaurant. Billy should go back, too, but he wasn't up for it, and he hoped his mother would understand. She was the one who'd organized this, after all.

"What happened?" Jude asked again.

"I freaked out. I'm not in love with Robin, but I thought it didn't matter. I found out it did. I couldn't marry him, not when he's not what I'm looking for and when I'm not what he thought I was."

Jude slowly nodded. "I see. Do you have to go back inside? Your mom didn't tell me why you were here, just that you would be."

"I was meeting her boyfriend and his children."

Jude gaped. "Maris has a boyfriend?"

"She does. It's fairly recent, from what she's been telling me, but it's serious."

"It has to be, if you're meeting him. You said he has children?"

"Three of them, all adults. And no, I don't have to go back inside. I'm pretty sure my mom knows I'm not up to it anymore. She's the one who told you where to find me, so she had to imagine I would want to talk to you. Either that, or that you'd kill me, and either way, I wouldn't be able to get back to the dinner."

Jude hooked an arm around Billy's shoulders. "I'm not going to kill you, although I was sorely tempted for a while. I'm still angry, too. But you're my best friend, and I want to listen to what you have to say before I make decisions, especially decisions that are so drastic."

"I don't want to tell you," Billy murmured. "I'm ashamed of the way I behaved." And not just when it came to Robin.

Jude was right. Billy shouldn't have limited himself to texting that he was okay. It didn't mean anything. He hadn't thought about what other people would feel when he left, but he should have. He'd been selfish, something he never wanted to be when it came to his family. "I should have told you what was going on, or at the very least, that I was leaving town," he admitted.

Jude sighed. "You should have, but we both know what I would have done if you had."

"You would have tried to convince me to go to Robin anyway."

"Because you need to talk to him. What you did wasn't right, Billy. You abandoned him without even telling him you were okay. Couldn't you have done this sooner? Why did you have to wait until you and Robin were about to get married?"

"You'll be the first to know if I ever find the answer to that."

"Let's go home to your mom's apartment. I want you to tell me everything, no matter how ashamed you are. You already disappointed me, and I doubt anything you can say will make that worse."

Billy grimaced. "Way to make me feel better."

"I wasn't trying to. You shouldn't feel better, not when Robin is still destroyed. I tried to reassure him and tell him that you'd gone back to your mom's place, but he didn't understand. He asked me so many questions I couldn't answer, and I felt like shit. That's on you, and you're going to fix it, whatever that means. I might be your best friend, but I care about Robin, too, and you've hurt him enough."

Billy's stomach churned. Now that Jude was here, he couldn't act as if everything was okay anymore. He might be able to lie to his mother, but he wouldn't be able to do the same with Jude.

He wouldn't bother trying.

CHAPTER FOUR

Niall couldn't stop thinking about Billy, and he had no idea why. It didn't make sense. He didn't even like Billy. They'd barely talked until their family dinner, and even then, they hadn't said more than a few words to each other. None of those words had been nice, which didn't even make them friendly, let alone friends, or anyone Niall should continue thinking about even when he was in his bed at night.

The problem was that he wasn't in his bed but at work, and obsessing over Billy wasn't going to help with his focus. He'd almost nailed his finger to the wall, which was when he'd realized Billy was becoming a problem.

Who was that guy Billy had been standing with? When he'd arrived, he'd been pissed, so much so that Niall had almost stepped in. The only reason he hadn't was that Flynn had stopped him. He'd told Niall to give it time, and sure enough, Billy and the guy had ended up hugging. They were obviously close, and Niall thought maybe the guy was Billy's ex-boyfriend.

It would make sense. Billy had been cagey about his break-up, and while Niall understood not wanting to give details to people he barely knew, maybe things between him and his ex weren't bad after all. Maybe the next time they had a family dinner, the boyfriend would be there, too. Niall didn't know how he would deal with that or if he would have to.

Something poked him in the ass, and he jerked around, glaring at Val. He was standing behind Niall, holding his hammer and using that to poke at him.

"What do you want?" Niall asked, trying not to snap.

Val put his hammer away, but he didn't leave. Instead, he crossed his arms over his chest and stood staring at Niall. "I thought that now that you know your father isn't ill, you'd be more focused at work."

Niall sighed. "I'd hoped so, too. Trust me. I wouldn't be distracted if I had a choice."

"What's going on this time?"

"Nothing."

Val snorted. "That's bullshit. You can tell me if you don't want to talk about it, but don't lie to me."

Niall *didn't* want to talk about it. Still, he found himself blurting out words he suspected were better kept to himself. "It's Maris's son. I met him the other night when we had dinner together, and he's an asshole. Did you know he almost ran me over with his car the first time we met?"

"I didn't, but I bet you made sure he remembered it when you met him the second time."

"Damn right, I did. It was dangerous, and I was lucky to notice the car before he hurt me. And you know what he did when we met at dinner? He said he was *overwhelmed*. He almost ran me over because he was *overwhelmed*. Can you believe that? And he didn't even stay at dinner. He left midway through, and he never came back, and his mother had to apologize for him."

"So he's rude. What does it have to do with you?"

Niall threw his hands in the air. "I don't know. I don't like how rude he is, even to his mother. That dinner was supposed to help our two families get to know each other, but instead, he left. How are we supposed to get to know him if he's not there? And even during when he was present, he barely looked at me."

"Maybe you did something to offend him?"

"I should have been the one offended after he almost ran

58

me over."

"With his car, yes, you already mentioned that."

Niall narrowed his eyes at Val. "What?" His best friend sounded amused, and Niall didn't understand how the situation warranted that reaction.

"Nothing. It sounds like maybe you're interested in that guy, though. What's his name?"

Niall spluttered. "I'm not interested in Billy." That was a lie, but Val didn't have to know it. The problem was that he'd always been able to read Niall much better than anyone else.

"You're sure? Because he's not the first rude guy you've met, yet I don't remember you ranting about any of them like you just did with Billy."

"We hate each other. It's not only the car thing. I told you he ignored me at dinner."

"And I suspect you know why he did that. How did you behave when you saw him?"

"I made sure he knew I remembered the almost accident." Val stared at Niall until Niall sighed. "Fine. Maybe he ignored me because I was rude. I shouldn't have confronted him the way I did."

"There you have it. Maybe it's not hate. Maybe you just don't know how to be around each other."

"How could we know if he left midway through?"

Val was still staring and making Niall uncomfortable. He wanted Val to say something, to agree with him when he said Billy was rude and shouldn't have left. It didn't matter that maybe he'd reconciled with his boyfriend. Niall didn't like that idea, even though he didn't know why.

"What's going on?" Val asked. "And I'm serious right now. There's something there, and while you don't have to tell me, I'm still your best friend."

"This doesn't have anything to do with our friendship. I just don't like Billy."

"I mean, you've always been prickly, but you don't usually hate people you don't know. Even when they're rude to you, you at least give them a chance. You're not giving Billy one, and I'm starting to think there's something more here, something you're not telling me."

Niall raked a hand through his hair. "Would you believe me if I told you that I don't like that Billy left in the middle of dinner, and I want to know why he did? I want to know who that guy he was talking to in the parking lot is, if he's his boyfriend or someone else. I want to know why he was overwhelmed the day he almost ran me over."

Val's eyes had gone wide, and Niall knew he'd said too much. He couldn't take it back, no matter how much he wanted to. "You like him," Val accused.

Niall bristled. "I never said I liked him. Did you hear me complain about him for the past ten minutes?"

"I did, and I thought it was strange. You're a complainer, but usually you don't stick to one person that way. You complain about everything, yet today, you're only complaining about Billy. It's almost as if you can't stop thinking about him."

"I can't," Niall admitted. He was frustrated. He didn't *want* to think about Billy. He wanted his brain to be free of the man, but he couldn't seem to make that happen. "I don't understand what's happening. I barely talked to him, and both times we met, we were rude to each other. He's cute, but I don't even know if he's interesting. What's going on?"

Val frowned. "And you're sure you didn't know him before?"

"I'm sure. He doesn't even live in town most of the time. He lived with his boyfriend, and now they broke up, and he came back. Maybe they're going to get back together. They looked okay when I saw them in the parking lot."

There was nothing Niall disliked more than being in the

dark, especially when he was involved. That was why he'd freaked out when he'd thought his father was hiding something. He didn't expect people to tell him all their secrets, but he wanted to know what was going on. This thinking about Billy, barely being able to focus on anything else, was a problem he wanted to solve, and he suspected he wouldn't be able to until he talked to Billy.

He wasn't about to do that. Billy clearly didn't want to talk to him, and Niall could hold a grudge like the best of them. Still, he and his siblings, along with his father, were supposed to have dinner with Billy and his mother tonight. That meant Niall wouldn't be able to avoid Billy, but also that Billy wouldn't be able to avoid him. Niall might not get answers, but this time, he promised himself he would try to be nice. At least that way, if Billy continued to be rude, Niall could say it wasn't his fault.

"I don't know what to do now," Billy murmured.

It was late in the morning, but he and Jude were still in bed. They were sharing, just like when they were younger in college, and thankfully Billy's mom hadn't said anything about it. She knew how important Jude was to Billy, and that it didn't mean anything more than friendship. Billy had almost cried when Jude had slipped into the bed with him after the disaster of a dinner with Regan and his family.

After he'd seen his mate.

Billy had been trying to understand how to untangle the situation since the dinner, but he was still lost, even after a few days. He hadn't talked to Robin, and he hadn't seen Niall again. His mother had been avoiding him, but hopefully, she was just giving him space and time. It wouldn't last forever, but it was nice not to have to answer to her.

Of course, Billy had to answer to Jude now.

His best friend was staring at him. He was waiting for Billy to do the right thing finally, but Billy was still terrified, and knowing that his mate was out there, so close that Billy would be able to talk to him later today, didn't help.

Billy sighed. "Okay. I do know what to do, at least when it comes to Robin."

"Finally," Jude snarked.

Billy wanted to hit him, but instead, he closed his eyes. "It's going to be a disaster, isn't it?"

"Not any worse than what's already going on. You were the one who created the disaster. You're going to try to fix it, and even though I don't expect miracles, both you and Robin need closure."

Billy hadn't told Jude that Niall was his mate. He hadn't told anyone. He wasn't ready to do that or to complicate the situation even more than it already was. He had no idea what his mother or Jude would say about Niall, but he'd wanted a few days to wrap his mind around that fact. He'd had those few days, and he didn't feel like anything had changed. He was still panicky, and he still had no idea what to do with this information. Jude would probably know, but to get his help, Billy would have to tell him, and he didn't want to.

Instead of obsessing over Niall, Billy sat up in his bed. He pulled the comforter higher on his chest, wrapping it around himself. It almost felt like a shield that would help him get through this, even though it was only fabric. It belonged to his childhood, to a time where everything had been easier. If it helped him, he wasn't going to push it away.

Jude sat up, too, leaning closer to Billy as Billy reached for the nightstand and took his phone. Having Jude here helped. Even though Jude wasn't saying anything, their shoulders brushed together every so often, and it reminded Billy that he wasn't alone. Whatever happened with Robin, he never would be. His mother wasn't going anywhere, and after the past few days, he didn't think Jude was, either.

Jude had told him what had happened after he'd left. Billy felt even more ashamed about abandoning Robin that way, but he couldn't do anything to fix it. He'd made his mistake, and he had to man up to it, which was what he was finally doing.

Robin hadn't gone on the honeymoon. Instead, he'd canceled everything. Billy didn't expect him to answer, but he still turned his phone on to call him. He ignored the emails and messages that reached him as soon as it was on, dialing Robin's number from memory. He took a deep breath, then hit the green button and raised the phone to his ear.

It rang. That was the first surprise. Robin hadn't blocked Billy, but then he wasn't the kind of person who would block anyone. He no doubt wanted to hear from Billy and make sure he was okay, which made Billy want to squirm. He'd never deserved a man like Robin, and he showed that once more.

"It's good to know you're not dead in a ditch," Robin drawled when he answered.

Billy was so stunned that for a few moments, he couldn't say anything. "Robin?" he asked.

"You called my number. Who did you expect?"

"I didn't think you'd answer, to be honest."

"I almost didn't."

"I'm so sorry for everything. I don't know what happened. One moment, I was driving toward you, and the next, I was coming to Green Hill. I panicked."

"I can understand panic, at least partially. What I don't understand is why you turned your phone off and disappeared from the face of the earth for so long. What's going on, Billy? Why did you run, and why did you ignore me for days? Do you know what I went through? I'm not even talking about the wedding, by the way. It was horrible to stand there waiting for you and have everyone stare at me while I realize you weren't coming, but it was even worse to think you had an accident and that you were dead somewhere."

Billy sucked in a breath. "I did all of this wrong. I should have talked to you before we got to the wedding day."

Robin was silent for a moment. "So you knew you didn't want to marry me, yet you didn't say anything."

"I did want to marry you. I love you, and I always will. You're such an important part of my life, and I don't know what I'll do without you."

"But I wasn't enough." Robin's voice had softened.

"Not you, but what we shared," Billy confirmed. "I don't feel the same for you as I did when we first met. I'm not in love with you anymore, but I didn't want to lose you. I knew that telling you that and not marrying you would push you away, and I was terrified."

Robin snorted. "So instead, you stood me up the day of our wedding and disappeared. You created the exact situation in which I would push you away and you would lose me."

"I didn't mean to. If I could change things, I would."

"But it's too late." Robin sighed. "I don't know if I can forgive you. You should have talked to me sooner, and while it would have hurt, it would have been nothing next to what you actually put me through. I hate you for what you did. I wish I never had to see you again or talk to you, but I know it's not reasonable."

"I don't think anyone expects you to be reasonable in this situation," Billy pointed out.

"Shut up. I don't care what people expect from me. I only care about what you did and the situation we're in right now. Are you coming home? Because I've been waiting here, and I didn't know what to do."

"I think I'm going to stay with my mother for a bit. Part of me wants to come home and be with you again, but I know it's only because I don't want to change anything."

"I'm not taking you back," Robin said bitterly. "If you're coming home, it's only to get your stuff. I was tempted to start packing it, but it was too much work."

"I'm sorry," Billy said. He'd probably said those words hundreds of times since he'd arrived in Green Hill, but they still felt like ash on his tongue.

"I know. I'm sorry, too," Robin said, and now, he sounded tired and nothing more. "I wish you'd have told me before, and I don't like that you couldn't. That's on me."

"All of this is on *me*. You didn't do anything."

"And that's the problem, isn't it? I should have known you didn't want to go through with the wedding. I could tell you were hesitant, but I still pushed. I thought you'd change your mind once we were married. I suppose I should count myself lucky that you left before we did. That way, we don't have to pay for lawyers and a divorce."

Billy pressed his lips together. He felt like he was about to cry, but he didn't want to. The only one who should cry here was Robin, but Billy knew he wouldn't, not on the phone with him anyway. "I'll let you know when I'm coming back for my things."

"Thank you. I'll make sure not to be home when you do."

Bill's heart broke a little more at those words, but what had he expected? He'd broken Robin's heart. It was only fitting that Robin broke his now.

Niall was bothered. Even though he'd talked to Val, he still didn't know how to behave with Billy, and he was about to spend another dinner with him. Billy might even stick around, but Niall had no idea how to feel about Billy except conflicted, which didn't help.

Maybe Billy wouldn't be rude today. Niall had promised

himself he would be careful about what he said to Billy and how he behaved, so it wouldn't be his fault if something happened. For some reason, that didn't make Niall feel as good as it should.

He'd arranged to meet with his siblings in front of the apartment building where Maris lived. He shuffled from foot to foot, waiting for them and wishing he had something to do with his hands. Maybe there was something to smoking, although he would never start, not after what had happened to his mother. He didn't understand how Flynn and Shona could smoke, even though their mother's cancer had nothing to do with that. He wasn't their father, though, and he couldn't order them around, no matter how much he wished he could in this situation.

He saw Flynn arrive and park his car, and as soon as Flynn was out, Niall waved at him. Flynn blinked, then came forward, looking Niall up and down. "I wasn't sure you'd come," he said.

Niall frowned. "Maris invited me, too. Why shouldn't I come?"

"Maybe because you looked like you wanted to either strangle or fuck her son?"

Niall spluttered. "What are you talking about?"

"Don't think I'm the only one who noticed. Shona and I talked about it, and we agreed that there's something between you and Billy."

"He almost killed me with his car!"

"Then maybe you want to strangle him. I'm not so sure, though. I think there's something more, and I wish you'd tell me."

"I promise, there's nothing. The dinner was the second time I talked to Billy, and the first time was when he almost killed me. I haven't heard from him since, and I wouldn't know where to find him even if I wanted to see him."

Flynn arched a brow and gestured at the building they were standing in front of. "How about his mother's apartment?"

"Billy and I have nothing to do with each other. I swear."

"I feel like you're protesting too much, but fine. I'll act as if I believe you. I want to be the first to know something is going on, though. It's not fair that Shona is always the one who does."

"Have you thought that maybe it's because she's nicer than you?"

"We both know that's a lie."

Luckily — or maybe not so luckily — they were interrupted by Shona. Her eyes glittered, and when she opened her mouth, Niall decided to cut her off before she could say something that would embarrass him.

"Ready to go upstairs?" he asked, trying to keep a cheery voice.

Shona blinked in confusion. "You didn't even say hello," she pointed out.

"Right. Hello. Ready to go upstairs?"

"Are you that eager to see Billy again?"

And there was what Niall had been trying to avoid. "I'm not eager to see him. He almost killed me the first time we met, and he was rude the second time. I want nothing to do with him."

"I think you're protesting too much."

That caused Flynn to start laughing, and when he explained why, Shona laughed, too. Niall glared at both of them, then turned around and headed toward the building. He didn't have to listen to his siblings laugh at him, did he?

Thankfully, they calmed down by the time they reached Maris's door. Niall still felt unsure, but there was no coming back from this, so he raised his hand and knocked on the door.

It swung open only seconds later, and Niall's father stood

there. He was beaming, which told Niall that he was doing the right thing. Whatever happened with Billy, Niall's father came first. He was happy with Maris, and Niall hoped that would continue. He would never do anything to cause them to break up, which included being rude to Maris's son. He was going to have to be the bigger man. He would apologize to Billy, and hopefully, it would be enough to smooth out whatever was going on between them.

"It's great to see you," Niall said, hugging his father.

"I'm excited the three of you agreed to come tonight."

Niall moved away so Shona and Flynn could say hello. "Why wouldn't we have? Maris invited us, so of course we came."

"I wasn't sure, since you and Billy seemed to be clashing the last time we did this."

So Niall's father *had* noticed. "It was a misunderstanding. We're over it."

Niall's dad didn't seem convinced, but thankfully, he didn't push. Instead, he closed the door behind Niall and his siblings and guided them into the apartment. It was nice, cozy, and lived in, exactly the kind of place Niall loved. He looked around, already smiling, until his gaze stopped on Billy. Then, the smile turned to a scowl that Niall tried his hardest to erase. He'd decided he would be the bigger man, so he strode toward Billy, offering him his hand. The fact that Billy leaned back as if afraid of Niall didn't help, though.

"I wanted to apologize for the way I reacted when I saw you last time, at the restaurant," Niall said.

Billy stared at Niall. "I seem to remember it was warranted."

Niall still had his hand extended, and he was starting to get pissed. "It might have been, but I still shouldn't have been rude. Why don't we start over?"

Billy finally shook Niall's hand, but it was tentative, and

Niall didn't know what to make of it. He'd apologized. What more did Billy want from him? Whatever it was, Niall had taken the first step, and Billy would have to take the next one.

They gathered in the living room with drinks. Niall kept looking at Billy, expecting him to smile or chat, but Billy stuck close to his boyfriend, who Niall now knew was Jude. They'd been introduced, and while Jude had seemed curious, he hadn't explained what his relationship with Billy was, so Niall could only assume.

He and Billy stood on the other side of the living room even now, leaning against each other as they talked. Niall had been dismissed, and for some reason, it made him angry. He'd decided he wouldn't make a scene, but would it kill Billy to be nice? He was obviously avoiding Niall, and Niall didn't know what to make of it. He'd apologized. There was nothing else he could do, but as time passed, his anger grew.

When he noticed Billy step away from his boyfriend and head into the hallway, Niall quickly put down his drink and followed him. Flynn looked startled at how their conversation was cut short, but Niall told him he needed to use the bathroom, and Flynn didn't argue.

Niall rushed into the hallway before he lost Billy. The apartment wasn't big, but it wouldn't do for him to stick his nose around. Thankfully, Billy was there, headed deeper down the hallway. Niall rushed toward him, ignoring Billy's soft cry of surprise when Niall grabbed his arm. Niall looked around. He didn't want to do this in the hallway where anyone could stumble onto them, so he pulled Billy toward the closest door, opening it and dragging him inside before he could realize it was a closet.

"Why did you just push me back into the closet?" Billy drawled.

Niall's cheeks felt warm, but thankfully, the closet was dark. Niall felt around for a light switch, and when his fingers hooked onto it, he flipped it. Both he and Billy blinked. "I wanted to talk to you," Niall said.

"And you had to drag me into a closet to do that?" Billy had sounded amused earlier, but now, he sounded irritated.

"I didn't have a choice. You've been avoiding me, and I didn't know how else to get you to talk to me."

"Dragging me in here isn't going to help. Can you do this like a normal person and try to talk to me in the living room?"

"I did, but you haven't stepped away from Jude." Niall glared. "Now tell me why you're avoiding me and why you're so rude." He wouldn't leave this closet before he had an answer, and if he had anything to say about it, neither would Billy.

Billy didn't want to be close to Niall. It made things even more confusing for him, and he couldn't deal with that right now. The closet was small, and it was filling with Niall's scent. It was driving Billy and his goat side crazy, and he hoped neither of them would do anything stupid. The way things were going, they probably would, and he wanted to go back to his bedroom to hide.

"I'm not going to talk to you in here," he said, reaching for the door.

Niall grabbed Billy's wrist before he could touch the handle and pulled him back. To Billy's surprise, he didn't let go. "I want to know what your problem with me is," Niall said.

"Have you thought that maybe it's that you're a rude asshole?"

"*You* were the one who almost killed me."

Billy tried to throw his hands in the air, but one was still in Niall's hold. "I already apologized for that, and I didn't try to kill you. It was an accident. I was overwhelmed and not focused on driving, and it was a mistake."

"At least you admit that. What else?"

"Nothing," Billy said through gritted teeth. He was trying hard not to breathe, because he got a nose-full of Niall's scent every time he did. It was getting harder to stay away from him, and Billy had to consciously move back when he found himself leaning closer to get a better sniff.

Niall gently shook Billy's arm. "That's bullshit. If it was only that, you would have talked to me at the restaurant and here. Instead, you're staying away from me. Why? Did I do something to offend you?"

"Dragging me into a closet can do that."

"You were already angry at me before I did. I want to know why." Niall paused, and when he started talking again, he sounded more hesitant. "I don't know what's going on, and I realize it's not my business. I want us to get along, though. I haven't seen my father this happy since my mother died, and I don't want to cause him and your mother problems. They're perfect together, and I won't ruin their relationship by bickering with you."

Billy tried to ignore the niggle of doubt in the back of his mind. Surely, he wasn't ruining his mother's relationship? He hadn't been trying to, and like Niall, he didn't want to. He also didn't want to spend any length of time in a closet with Niall. If this continued, he would do or say something he wasn't supposed to, and Niall would realize they were mates. There was no way for Billy to know how Niall would react, and he wasn't ready to face that conversation, not after he talked to Robin today.

"I agree they're perfect together," he said. "I don't know what you want from me, though. I'm not your best friend, but then we just met. What did you expect?"

"For you to at least look at me and talk to me."

"Well, we just had a conversation in a closet. Is that enough talking for your taste?" Billy snarked. He didn't wait for Niall to answer, reaching for the door again. He needed out, and he needed it to happen *now*.

Niall had other plans. He pulled Billy back again, harder this time, and Billy stumbled onto a boot that was on the floor. He tilted forward, but thankfully, Niall caught him. He had to let go of Billy's wrist to do that, and he wrapped his arms around Billy.

Billy tilted his head to thank Niall—he wasn't that much of an asshole that he wouldn't—and froze. He was wrapped in his mate's scent, and he wanted nothing more than to lean even closer and kiss Niall. He couldn't move, though. Kissing Niall would be the worst thing he could do right now, and he wasn't ready to fuck up his life even more than he already had.

Niall took the decision out of Billy's hands. He leaned forward, pressing even closer to Billy. He was only a few inches shorter, and they fit together perfectly when they kissed. Niall's lips were a bit chapped, but it still felt like heaven. Niall was warm and gentle, as if he was trying to coax Billy into kissing him back.

Billy did. He couldn't have said no, not even if the door had opened. He'd wanted to kiss Niall since the first time he'd seen him, even though he'd almost killed him. He'd been angry, and Niall was infuriating on the best of days as far as Billy was concerned, but that didn't mean he didn't want him.

Then Billy's brain kicked back into gear. He realized what they were doing—kissing in a closet, for fuck's sake—and tried to step back. The closet was small, and his back hit the wall. Niall moved closer, maybe to kiss Billy again, but Billy didn't think he could stand that. Panic was freezing his brain, and he could only think about getting away. Niall was blocking his way to the door, so Billy did the only thing he could think about.

He shifted.

It wouldn't have been a problem at any other time, but Billy was overwhelmed with feelings and insecurities, and he was a fainting goat shifter. The fact that Niall seemed shocked to see him shift didn't help, either. As soon as Billy was in his goat form, the world around him turned dark as he fainted.

Billy groaned when he woke up. He wiggled his toes and fingers, relieved to see he was in his human form. He had no idea what had happened, but he was lying on his back, and he was pretty sure he was on his bed. There was no way the closet floor was so comfortable.

He cracked open an eye, hoping he wasn't about to find Niall staring down at him. Thankfully, he didn't. Instead, both Jude and Billy's mother were standing there, murmuring. There was no sign of Niall or anyone of his family, and Billy relaxed.

"What happened?" he asked, pulling the blanket tighter around his naked body.

Jude rushed closer, taking one of Billy's hands. "How are you feeling?"

Billy shrugged Jude's hand away and sat up. "You've already seen me faint for no reason. Don't worry. I'm fine."

"Are you sure?"

"I am."

His mother sat at the foot of the bed and wrapped her fingers around one of Billy's ankles. "What happened?"

"I'm not sure." That was a lie, but Billy wasn't ready to tell them what had truly happened just yet. "I'm sorry I ruined your dinner."

She waved his words away with her free hand. "Don't worry about it. Although I suppose this sets a precedent. Every time you and I get together with Regan's family, something happens. I'm starting to think it's not such a good idea."

That was the last thing Billy wanted. "Don't break up with

him because of that. I swear there's an explanation."

Her eyebrows flew up. "I sure hope there is, but I'm not about to break up with Regan because of this. I'd like that explanation, though."

Billy rubbed his face with both his hands. "What happened?"

"We're not sure," Jude answered. "We were in the living room when Niall rushed in, carrying you. You were in your goat form. He said you'd shifted and had fainted." Jude pressed his lips together.

Billy could see he wanted to laugh, but he didn't, and Billy was glad. He could only imagine the scene he and Niall had made, and he would find it hilarious in any other situation.

"He didn't know about fainting goats," Billy's mother continued. "Was he bothering you? Is that why you shifted?"

It would be easy to say yes, but Billy didn't want Niall to get in trouble, especially when he'd done nothing to warrant it. "Not exactly. He wanted to talk to me about why I've been rude to him, and he dragged me into the closet in the hallway."

Billy's mom gasped, while Jude looked like Christmas had come early. "What did he say?" Jude asked.

Billy was going to have to tell them, wasn't he? He didn't want to, but he felt like now was the right moment. "He asked me what I had against him, and I couldn't answer. He kissed me, I freaked out, shifted, and fainted. You know the rest."

"What do you have against him?"

Billy sighed. "Nothing. This just wasn't the best moment in my life to meet my mate, and that's who he is."

CHAPTER FIVE

No matter how hard he tried not to think about it, Niall couldn't get the image of Billy fainting out of his mind. He couldn't believe he'd caused something that to happen. Was he such a bad kisser?

He shook his head. He had to stop being an idiot. He knew that Billy fainting had nothing to do with the kiss, or rather, that it had nothing to do with how Niall kissed. But clearly, Billy had been overwhelmed, and now Niall had to find a way to make him feel better.

After he'd carried Billy into the living room where both their families were gathered, he, his father, and his siblings had left. Maris had insisted that Billy would be okay and pointed out that they were fainting goat shifters, but Niall had no idea what that meant. He'd never heard of fainting goats, and he was still worried. The fact that Jude had tried to reassure him, too, hadn't helped.

Niall wondered if Jude was with Billy now. Probably, since they were a couple. Jude was no doubt used to Billy fainting and knew what to do to make him feel better. Niall, on the other hand, would no doubt make things worse if he tried to help. He was the one who'd made Billy faint, after all.

He still wanted to know what had happened and to apologize. That was the only reason he was standing in front of Maris's apartment building now. He looked up, wondering if Billy was home. He knew Billy needed to rest and relax, and what better place to do that than somewhere you could be with your mother and your boyfriend? They might kick Niall out when he knocked on their door, since he was the cause of Billy's fainting, but he hoped he would be able to apologize before it happened.

With a sigh, he walked into the building.

He hadn't expected the other night to go the way it had, especially after he and Billy had kissed. It had been a surprise, although maybe it shouldn't have. The way they'd been bickering pointed at either that or that they hated each other, and no matter how much Niall insisted he disliked Billy, he truly didn't. He disliked the fact that Billy wouldn't give him the time of day, but he needed to stop acting like an asshole, especially after his latest conversation with Val. Niall suspected there was more than he was aware of between him and Billy, and he wanted to find out if he was right.

Which was one of the reasons he was here. He hoped to apologize and clear things out between him and Billy so that the next time they had a family dinner, things would go the right way. Hopefully, the third time would be a charm.

He made his way to Maris's apartment. Once he was in front of the door, he paused, listening. He could hear the faint sound of the TV on, so hopefully, someone was home. He didn't think Billy had left, not when he should be resting, but who could know? What had happened had highlighted just how little he knew Billy and shifters in general. If he'd known more, he might have been able to help.

He knocked and waited. When the door swung open, he wasn't surprised to see Jude standing on the other side, although he would have preferred Maris. Jude's eyes widened, causing Niall to take a step back for no good reason. Jude was tall but slim like Billy, so Niall had no reason to fear him, although he'd seen thin guys kick-ass before. He supposed he should be careful not to anger him either way.

Niall cleared his throat. "I was wondering if I could talk to Billy?"

"Of course."

Niall hadn't expected Jude to agree so readily.

Jude looked around. "Actually, I should probably go for a walk. That way, the two of you can clear the air without someone hovering over your shoulder."

"I didn't mean to send you running." Still, Niall couldn't say that he wasn't satisfied at the thought of having Billy to himself.

Jude shook his head. "You're not sending me running. You and Billy need to talk, and it's better if you do it on your own."

"Is he okay after what happened? Because if he's not, I could come back another time."

Jude waved Niall's words away. "He's fine. You should get used to his fainting if you're going to be in his life."

"I'd never heard of fainting goats."

"I hadn't either until I met him. He'll tell you all about it, though." Jude quickly smiled at Niall as he stepped back to let him in. "He's in the living room. You know the way. Just tell him I had to leave for a bit. I'll be back in about fifteen to twenty minutes. That should give you time to talk things out." Jude hesitated. "Good luck. I know you don't owe Billy anything, but he's a mess right now, so go easy on him, huh?"

Niall watched Jude step out of the apartment and close the door behind himself. He hadn't expected any of this, but he would make the most of it.

He turned around, headed toward the living room. Jude hadn't mentioned Maris, but Niall didn't think she was home since Jude had mentioned Billy and Niall talking on their own. If she was, well, it didn't matter. He wasn't here to kiss Billy again or to make him uncomfortable. He was here to apologize, and if something else happened, he wouldn't complain, but that wasn't his main goal.

He found Billy on the couch, watching TV. He was curled up under a blanket and his focus was on the screen, but he looked up when he heard Niall. When he saw him, he scrambled into a sitting position, looking around frantically. "Where's Jude?" His hair was messy. Niall wondered if it was because he'd been napping or because he and Jude had been making out.

Niall gestured toward the entrance. "He went out."

Billy scowled. "He's never been able to keep his nose out of things that aren't his business." He sighed and settled back against the couch. "Do you want to sit down?"

Niall didn't, not when the only spot where he could sit down was on the couch next to Billy, but he wasn't going to refuse what seemed like an olive branch. He and Billy had to work things out—whatever that meant—for both their parents' sake. Even if they could never be friends or anything more, they had to be at least civil to each other.

Niall gingerly sat on the edge of the couch, as far as possible from Billy as he could, and twisted to look at him. Billy seemed both amused and annoyed, and when he caught Niall looking at him, he arched a brow. "You do know I don't bite, right? I'm a goat shifter, not a tiger."

Niall's cheeks felt warm. "I'm aware."

"So, why are you here?"

"I wanted to apologize for what happened."

Billy blinked. "What do you mean?"

"I caused you to faint. I don't know what happened exactly, but it's obvious it had to do with me, and I'm sorry."

Billy continued staring.

It made Niall uncomfortable, but he stayed where he was, wondering if Billy had questions.

"What do you know about fainting goats?" Billy finally asked.

Niall snorted. "I didn't even know they existed until last night."

That seemed to amuse Billy. "Well, we're an American

breed. The breed's main characteristic is that we're afflicted by a hereditary condition that causes us to stiffen and fall over when we're startled. It's not really fainting, although I *did* faint last night. I was overwhelmed, and everything caught up to me at the worst moment."

Niall rubbed the back of his neck. He had no idea what Billy was saying, except for the fact that Niall had overwhelmed him. "I shouldn't have kissed you."

Billy's expression twisted. "Are you saying that because you didn't want to kiss me, or because I fainted when you did?"

Niall had taken the time last night to think about it, so he knew the answer to Billy's question. Now was the time to be honest, even though he didn't like making himself vulnerable. "I wanted to kiss you, and if I could, I would do it again. What I did wasn't right, though, not when it made you faint. You were panicking, and I don't want people panicking because I kiss them."

Billy sighed. "I didn't panic because of the kiss, or at least, not entirely. It's a long story."

"Well, we're alone, at least for now. I can listen if you want to explain."

"I'm pretty sure I would bore you to death."

Niall didn't think he would. "I promise that if you bore me, I'll let you know. I truly do want us to be friendly, though. If not for our sake, for my dad's and your mom's. So again, I'm listening."

Niall wasn't sure it would be enough, but he'd taken the steps. Now Billy had to decide what he would do — tell Niall to fuck off and never show his face again, or try to talk to each other without snipping and making each other faint.

Billy didn't want to do this. He was already embarrassed

enough that he had to tell Niall about fainting goats. He wasn't sure Niall had understood what he was saying, but he hadn't asked questions, so Billy didn't provide answers. He was sure Niall could use the Internet if he was curious.

And now Niall wanted to know about Billy's life. Billy would have to tell him about Robin and what he'd done, which embarrassed him even more than fainting in front of his mate. There was also the fact that Billy should probably tell Niall they were mates. Now that they were talking instead of bickering, he liked Niall, and he realized he was wrong not to tell him about their bond. He'd been in the wrong too often lately, and he wanted that to change. It might finish pushing Niall away, or it might make him soften even more, which was something Billy hoped to see one day.

Billy had seen how Niall was with his father and his siblings. He was gentle and happy, and it was apparent he cared about them. Billy wanted that attention directed toward him, but he didn't know if what he was about to say would make that happen or make it impossible.

He twisted his fingers together as he looked down at them. "There's nothing much to say. I was supposed to get married a few weeks ago. Instead, I ran back to my mom's apartment."

"Why did Jude follow you? No offense, but I would have been pissed if you'd done something like that to me."

Billy frowned but answered. "He wanted to know what had happened to me. My mother told him where I was, although I'd texted him to tell him I was okay."

Niall snorted. When Billy looked at him, he waved. "Sorry. It's not funny, but you *texted* him to tell him you weren't going to marry him?"

It took Billy's brain a few moments to understand what Niall was saying. "Oh, I wasn't going to marry Jude. He's my best friend."

"Not your boyfriend?"

"We've never seen each other that way, thankfully." Because Billy was pretty sure he would have managed to lose Jude, too, if they'd been together. "My boyfriend's name is Robin. Well, my ex-boyfriend."

"Fiancé, you mean."

Billy glared. "My *ex*. His name is Robin, and I ran away from him and our wedding."

"So your relationship with him was serious."

"Very much so, at least in the beginning. I let things go too far, though." If there was one person who deserved to hear the entire story, it was Niall, no matter how uncomfortable it made Billy. "We were together a long time before we decided to get married. I never really thought about it, but it was something important to him, so I went along with it. I thought I would be more than happy to marry him, and I was, for a while."

"Yet you ran away," Niall said when Billy didn't continue.

"I didn't even mean to. I was headed to marry him, but instead, I started driving toward Green Hill. I panicked."

"You seem to do that often enough."

Billy glared, but he couldn't deny Niall was right. "I wanted to marry Robin. I didn't want my life to change and lose him, but I couldn't go through with it in the end. I love him, but I'm not *in* love with him, and I haven't been in a long time. Leaving was the right thing to do, but I went about it the wrong way, and I don't blame him for being angry."

"So he knows what happened to you now?"

"I called him yesterday. I should have done it sooner, but I wasn't ready. He knew I was here, though. Both my mother and Jude let him know."

Niall leaned back against the couch. He was more relaxed now, and he looked at home here. That made something flutter in Billy's stomach, but he did his best to ignore it. He couldn't allow his imagination to run wild just yet.

"That's a bit of a mess," Niall said.

"And that's an understatement. But yes, it's a huge mess. I didn't want my life to change, and now it's in shambles. I have to leave the apartment I lived in for years, I don't have a boyfriend anymore, and I'm probably going to have to find a new job here in Green Hill."

"Why? You could just find a new apartment. And I'm sure you can find a new boyfriend easily enough, although I realize you probably don't want to so soon after breaking up with Robin."

Niall had no idea Billy wasn't ever going to find another boyfriend. He'd met his mate. No one else could compare, no matter how much it annoyed him. "I want to move back home to Green Hill. It makes sense." Because both his mother and his mate were here.

Jude wasn't, though, but Billy supposed they would deal with that once they got to the point when they couldn't ignore it anymore. They were adults. They didn't have to live in each other's pockets the way they had since college.

Niall slowly nodded. "I see. Well, you made a mess, but it's not the end of the world. I'm sorry you lost someone important to you, though."

Billy rubbed his face. "Things would have been much easier if I'd taken the time to think instead of being an asshole. I ignored the signs until I couldn't anymore, which made a mess. I'm not going to do that again. Which is why I have to tell you something."

Niall frowned. "That doesn't sound good."

"I suppose it depends on what you expect and want. But first, I want to apologize for how antagonizing I've been to you."

"Don't. Now that I know what happened, I understand better why you were overwhelmed and snappish. I don't have the same excuse. I should have been the bigger man and let it go, but instead, I pushed. I'm sorry. I truly want things between us to go smoothly, whether or not you decide you want to see what might happen between us." His cheeks flushed. "Or we can just ignore the fact that we kissed. It doesn't have to mean anything, especially considering the rest of your situation."

Niall shouldn't be adorable, but he was when he blushed. It changed him from a grumpy, big man to one who looked as sweet as he actually was. Billy hadn't allowed himself to think about what would happen now that he'd found out he and Niall were mates, but maybe he should have. He didn't know what he wanted from Niall, but he supposed he wouldn't be the only one to make those choices. First, though, he had to tell Niall they were mates.

"Or it could mean something," he said slowly. He was cautious, even after what he and Niall had just said. Niall might change his mind once he found out he was linked to Billy, even though they weren't bonded. No matter what they decided, they would always be linked to each other. Niall might be able to ignore that since he was human, but Billy never would be able to, and the thought made him panic again.

What if Niall didn't want anything to do with him after he told him about their bond?

A touch on his hand startled Billy so hard he jerked back. Niall raised his hands, and when Billy just stared at him, he gently and slowly took Billy's hand again. "We don't have to make any kind of decision right now. I don't expect anything from you, and if you want me to apologize again for kissing you, I will. I'm not sorry I did, though, not when it hopefully showed you we might have something. You can take as much time as you want, as long as you tell me what's going on."

Billy swallowed and nodded. "I should tell you, yes." His mouth was dry, but he pushed through. "One of the reasons I panicked so much in the closet is that you're my mate."

Niall was relieved to know what was happening finally. He'd suspected something like this, but it was good to know for sure. "I see," he said slowly.

Truthfully, he'd had time to think about this and wrap his mind around the fact that he and Billy could be mates. He'd realized that what he felt for Billy was complicated and strange, and he'd talked about it with Val. Who better to understand how Niall felt than a man who was already with a shifter? Niall had explained how he felt, and even though Val hadn't been a hundred percent sure, he'd confirmed it was similar to how he'd felt about Simon. The only way for Niall to know for sure would have been to ask Billy, and now, he wouldn't have to.

Knowing they were mates didn't solve all their problems, though. If anything, it made the situation more complicated. Billy was still dealing with the ending of his old relationship and what he'd done, and Niall had no idea what to do with a mate. He'd been wary of shifters until recently, and while he wanted to embrace Billy and make him a part of his life, he couldn't help but wonder if it could work.

What did Billy want, anyway? He'd said he wasn't in love with his ex anymore, and that might be true, but the relationship still meant a lot to him. Could Niall compete with that — would he have to? Niall had a lot of questions, but no answers, although that might change. Billy was here, and he'd finally been honest. Hopefully, that meant he would answer most of the questions Niall had.

"This is when you're supposed to say something," Billy said.

Niall had been lost in his thoughts, but he wished he hadn't been. He knew how nervous Billy was, and it was apparent he expected Niall to reject him.

"I'm sorry," Niall said.

Billy shook his head. "Don't be. Just let me know what's going on. I know this is a lot to take, especially after what I just told you, but I thought you should know. I'm not the only one mixed up in this, after all."

Niall snorted. "That's an understatement. I'll be honest—I expected something like this to happen."

Billy stared. "You did?"

"I thought the way we behaved with each other was weird. I mean, I'm grumpy on the best of days, but I don't usually snap at people and hold a grudge." Niall paused. "Well, not most of the time." Niall supposed that eventually Billy would find out just how grumpy he was, but in the meantime, Niall hoped to make a good impression.

A better impression than he had until now anyway.

"And after we kissed," Niall continued, "I had no idea what was going on, but I knew I wanted to kiss you again, which didn't make sense."

"The bond didn't push you to kiss me, if that's what you're thinking. You might be drawn to me, but you can walk away."

"That's not what I meant. I guess you should probably get used to me making a mess of things and putting my feet in my mouth. It's not the first time I have, and I doubt it will be the last."

Billy laughed. It sounded good, light, and Niall suspected Billy sorely needed it. After everything, it wasn't a surprise.

"I suppose we can make a mess of things together," Billy gently teased.

Niall was relieved to see their relationship—if they were ever to have one—would go this way. He didn't want Billy to be meek and gentle, at least not all the time. He'd enjoyed bickering with him, and he could see them doing that for years to come.

First, though, they had to get over this initial hurdle. "Maybe we can," Niall agreed. "What I was trying to say is that I wanted to kiss you, and I didn't understand why. I liked you well enough once I could see past my grudge, I suppose, but with you always being rude to me, it didn't make sense that I wanted more."

Billy scowled and crossed his arms over his chest. "I wasn't rude." Niall arched a brow and stared at him until Billy huffed. "Fine. I *was* rude, but not all the time. Besides, you weren't exactly the picture of politeness, either."

"I never said I was. I apologize for that, too. We started on the worst foot, but I hope that now we can change that. I don't expect our relationship to be magically fixed, but I think that knowing what's going on between us will help."

Billy slowly nodded. "My mom told me you didn't like shifters." He sounded hesitant.

Niall could have kicked his past self for being an idiot about shifters. "That's not true. I understand why she might think that, though, especially if she talked to my father about it."

"So you like shifters?"

"I like *you*. But I'll admit I was wary of shifters because of the pride. They've been in Green Hill for decades, yet they were hidden, and barely anyone remembered they were even here. Now, there are shifters all over the place, and I don't know how to deal with that." Niall swallowed. Billy had been honest with him, and he wanted to be honest with Billy, too. "I was also annoyed that a shifter took my best friend away from me, in a way. Val and I have never been anything more than friends, but we used to spend a lot of time together. That changed when he met Simon, and while I don't begrudge him for it, I was annoyed."

"You're jealous."

"I was," Niall admitted. "I understand better what

happened now that I've met you and I know we're mates. He couldn't have stayed away from Simon even if he'd wanted to, and he didn't. He and Simon are happy, and I'm happy that they are."

"So you don't have anything against me because I'm a shifter?"

"I promise I don't. I found you intriguing even when I still thought you were infuriating and rude. Now that we talked, I want to make more of an effort. I think we should start again from the beginning and try to fix things between us as well as we can."

Billy stared at him for a moment before extending his hand. Niall glanced at it, not understanding. Billy huffed and said, "I'm Billy. It's a pleasure to meet you."

It was corny as hell, and Niall was pretty sure he'd seen this in a movie, but he still took Billy's hand and shook it. "The pleasure is mine. I think we'll be great friends."

Billy barked out a laugh. His hand was warm and dry in Niall's, and Niall gently squeezed. He was grateful Billy wasn't taking his hand away yet. They hadn't yet talked about what all of this meant for them as mates, but it would come.

"I hope we'll be more than friends," Billy said.

"I suppose we'll see what happens. I want you to know one thing, though, Billy." Niall was serious again, and he needed Billy to understand that. "Whatever I thought about shifters until now, it's in the past. You're my mate, and I won't have another one. This is a once-in-a-lifetime opportunity for me to be loved and to love someone in a way few people experience. I'm not going to waste it."

"You don't even know if we can be friends together, let alone more."

"Maybe not, and I'll admit that we didn't start in the best of ways, but we wouldn't be mates if we couldn't work."

"I suppose you're right, but I know this isn't going to be

easy. You have some baggage, and I have a lot of it."

"I don't think it'll matter in the long run, but if it makes you feel better, we can go as slow as you need and want." Niall had questions, and he hoped Billy wouldn't mind answering them, but that was where he'd stop pushing. Everything else would be on Billy's terms.

Billy had expected Niall to tell him to fuck off. Even if he'd done it in a way that wouldn't come off as rude, Billy would have been hurt. Instead, Niall was accepting him and their bond, and it was confusing.

Billy had been sure that between the dislike they had for each other and the whole story with Robin, Niall wouldn't want anything to do with him. He wouldn't have blamed him, either. He was a lot to deal with, especially in this situation.

Instead, Niall seemed to be understanding, and he was still holding Billy's hand.

Billy cleared his throat. Holding hands didn't mean anything. Niall might only be trying to reassure him, and this could be the only way he could think of doing it. Billy needed to focus on what was happening and on getting answers out of Niall. Right now, Niall sounded too good to be true, and Billy wanted to poke at it and make sure he actually was.

"Do you have any questions?" he asked softly. He wanted to hear them before they moved forward with their relationship, whatever it would be like.

"Just one."

"What is it?" Billy was ready to answer even the hardest ones. He'd hidden things from someone he loved once, and he wouldn't repeat the mistake.

"Will you faint every time we kiss?"

Billy found himself smiling, which was once again the last thing he'd expected. Maybe Niall would continue to surprise him. "I sure hope not. Does that mean you want to kiss me again?"

"Desperately, as long as you're sure you won't end up on the floor a second time."

Billy shook his head. "I wouldn't have fainted if I hadn't shifted. The fainting thing only happens when I'm in my goat form. As for why I shifted, well, I was panicking, and I couldn't find a way out of the room. You looked like you wanted to kiss me again when I stopped the first kiss, and it was the first thing I thought of that would make you stop."

Niall wrinkled his nose. "You're right about that. No offense, but I'm not into kissing goats." He cocked his head and looked at Billy. "Although I might make an exception for you. You're cute when you're a goat, even when you're unconscious."

Niall was going to be the end of Billy, wasn't he? No matter what he'd said about being wary of shifters, he seemed to be more than okay with the fact that Billy could turn into a goat.

"I have another question, actually," Niall said after a few moments.

"I already told you I would answer any question I could. Just ask them, and we'll go from there."

"What do you want from this?" Niall asked, gesturing between the two of them so Billy understood what he was talking about. "You just ended an important relationship. I can't imagine you're ready to embark on a new one."

Billy was surprised by the fact that he felt ready for more with Niall. It wasn't just that Niall was his mate, but also that he hadn't been in love with Robin for a long time. Now that he'd met Niall, he could feel those emotions growing already, and he knew it wouldn't take him long to fall in love.

The problem was that he was fragile and lost. He hadn't merely broken up with Robin and lost him. He'd also lost the place he'd called home for years, his job, and the city he'd lived in. He might have lost Jude in a way if he decided to stay there when Billy moved back to Green Hill. And why should Jude move to Green Hill? He didn't have anything here except Billy, and right now, Billy was pretty sure Jude thought he was a problem more than a necessity.

Billy was terrified he would do something stupid and disappoint Niall, too. He suspected he would feel this way for a while, after the mess he'd made of his relationship with Robin, and he wasn't entirely sure what he was ready to give Niall.

"I think that eventually, I want love with you," he said, his voice barely louder than a whisper. "We're mates, and I want us to bond. I want us to spend the rest of our lives together, making each other happy."

"And infuriating each other," Niall added.

He was smiling, and Billy relaxed even more. "And that, too. I don't think it's something we'll ever grow out of. But my life is a mess right now. I really want to move to Green Hill, and I think it's the thing that makes the most sense, both for me as an individual and for us as a couple. That means leaving everything I know behind, though, and dealing with how I feel about this place. When I was growing up, I always dreamed of leaving the town and never coming back, and I tried my hardest to make that happen. Coming back feels like a defeat, especially coupled with the end of my relationship with Robin."

Niall grimaced. "Those are complicated feelings."

"They are, but I want to get over them. I want a fresh start with you, but it's going to take a while. I also feel a bit broken, and I don't want you to have to fix me. I should be the one fixing myself."

"Even though I want to help as much as I can, I agree. Where do we go from here, then?"

"I think we should take things slow. I don't know much

about your life yet, but I can tell you're as hesitant as I am."

"I'm not sure about that, but I agree we should get to know each other and not expect anything yet. You have a lot to deal with, and maybe you're not the only one. My feelings for shifters are complicated, and even though I'm over my wariness, I still have work to do. I have people to apologize to, and that includes your mother. I didn't treat her the way I should have."

Billy leaned closer and kissed Niall's cheek. "From what I know, there was more to it than the fact that she's a shifter. You lost your mother, and it was traumatic. My mom doesn't expect you to be over it or to accept her with open arms."

"I should have, though. Yes, losing my mother hurt, and it still does to this day, but it's been ten years. My father deserves to be happy, and your mother does that for him." He frowned. "Isn't that going to be weird, though? Our parents are dating, and so are we."

Billy ignored the way his heart raced. "Is that what we're doing? Dating?"

Niall blushed again. Now that they were talking and that everything was on the table, Billy could stop resisting the urge to lean forward again and kiss the blush. It deepened, which made Billy chuckle. There were hidden depths in Niall, and he couldn't wait to discover all of them.

"I think we are," Niall answered. "I hope so, anyway. That's what getting to know each other is, right? People who date do it because they want to see if they can work together."

"I suppose you're right. And I don't think it will be weird. We're both adults, and it's not like we'll have to move in together once our parents do."

"I'm not sure I'm ready for them to do that, but I won't try to stop them if they decide to go that way. I also hope I'll be too distracted by you to care."

Billy grinned. "I promise I'll do everything I can to distract you."

"I have no doubt."

Then, since Billy had promised to distract Niall, he leaned closer. He made sure to give Niall the opportunity to move away if he didn't want to be kissed, but he was relieved when Niall didn't. This time, when their lips touched, Billy didn't freak out.

He still had no idea what was happening or what he would do with his life, but one thing he was sure of—Niall would be in his future, and right now, that was all that Billy could make himself care about.

CHAPTER SIX

Niall was jittery, but he was doing his best not to show it. He was pretty sure that at least Val had noticed something was up with him, though. He had to be annoyed considering how many times something had been up with Niall recently. For now, he hadn't asked for details, but Niall didn't hold his breath that he wouldn't eventually. Not that it would be a problem since Niall wanted to scream from the rooftops that he and Billy were mates and that they were trying to make things work as a couple.

If anyone had told him a few months ago that he would be happy at the thought of having a mate, he would have told them to fuck off. He still wasn't sure what had changed, although he suspected it was a mix of things. It was knowing Billy would never have another mate, and neither would Niall. It was seeing Niall's father with Maris, happy and finally smiling again after so many years. He didn't care that Maris was a shifter, and neither did Niall. Niall also didn't care that Billy was a shifter, not anymore.

The thought that Billy could turn into a goat whenever he wanted weirded out Niall a bit, but he'd decided to do his best to ignore that part of Billy, at least until he was more comfortable with it. The last thing he wanted was to make Billy feel unwelcome or for them to fight, especially since their relationship was so new. They were still trying to work things out, which was complicated with everything happening in Billy's life, and for once, Niall was more than happy to continue. If he and Billy were supposed to be together, they would be eventually.

That was what they were working toward, which was why Niall had a date with Billy tonight. It shouldn't make him feel like he was a teenager again, not when he was long past those years and used to dating, but he supposed that dating your mate did that to you. Billy wasn't just a guy. He wasn't even just a guy Niall liked. He was Niall's *mate*, and even though Niall wasn't a shifter, he'd seen how happy Val and Simon were. He wanted that, too, and while he hadn't expected it to happen with Billy, he was more than ready for the challenge.

"All right, I've had enough," Val said, putting down the brush he'd been using to paint the wall.

Niall continued painting, ignoring his best friend. He didn't want to make a big thing out of this, especially over just a date.

"Did you hear me?" Val asked. "I told you I'd had enough."

Niall sighed and put down his brush, too. He turned to face Val, grinning when he saw a streak of white down Val's cheek. "I'm not deaf, so yes, I heard you. I also have eyes, and you should clean up. You look like you've been painting your own face instead of the wall."

Val didn't answer. Instead, he cleaned his face with the bottom of his t-shirt. "Happy?"

"I'm sure Simon will be happy that he doesn't have to kiss paint."

"Enough talking about Simon and me. What's going on with you this time?"

"Would you believe me if I told you nothing?"

Val snorted. "Fat chance of that. I'm not an idiot."

"Would you let it go if I told you I didn't want to talk about it, then?"

Val crossed his arms over his chest and arched a brow.

Niall didn't have to ask twice. "I'm just nervous."

"That much was obvious. About what, though? Is it your father? Are he and Maris okay?"

"They're perfectly fine. And no, it's not them. It's Billy and me. We're going on a date tonight, and I'm not sure how to deal with that."

Val looked confused. "What do you mean you and Billy are going on a date?"

"Exactly what I said. We talked, and we agreed to take things slow, but we're dating."

"I know he's your mate, but you don't have to date him if you don't want to."

For some reason, something in Niall bristled. "Why wouldn't I want to date Billy?"

"Maybe because you hate him?" Val sounded hesitant, but he still said the words.

Niall couldn't blame him. He'd been complaining about how rude Billy had been since the first time they'd met, so of course Val would find it strange that Niall wanted to date him, even though they were mates. After all, Niall had made it obvious what he thought of shifters, and his mate was a shifter.

He'd really been an asshole, hadn't he? He was doing his best to fix it, but he wasn't sure he could or how to do it.

"I don't hate Billy," he explained. "I actually quite like him now that we've had the opportunity to talk. He told me what was going on in his life, and we realized that we were clashing because of the bond. I'm pretty sure that if it hadn't been there between us, I would have been able to walk away without thinking twice about him. Instead, I felt pulled toward him, and I acted like the stubborn asshole I am. He's dealing with a lot, so he did the same, which is why we ended up fighting or snapping at each other every time we met. That's over, though."

Val slowly shook his head. "I'll admit I wasn't sure what to think when you told me he was your mate, and I was afraid you would run him out of town without thinking twice about it. I'm glad to see that's not the case. Maybe you're growing up." He grinned. "It was about time, since you're almost forty."

Niall resisted the urge to flick paint at Val's face. He was trying to show his best friend he was an adult, after all. "Almost. I'm not yet forty, though, and I still have a few years until I reach that age. And if I'm honest, I don't quite know what to do with a shifter, but I suppose I'll find out soon enough."

Val rolled his eyes and grabbed his brush again. "You don't have to do anything different than when you date a human. They're shifters, not monsters or aliens. Part of them is as human as you and I are, and it's that part you have to woo. Usually, their animal parts are more than on board with bonding with their mates."

Niall would have to talk to Billy about this. He wanted to know more about shifters and what he should expect, although maybe a first date wasn't the right moment to ask. He should make a list of questions so he would know what to ask when they grabbed lunch or something.

Or maybe not. Maybe he should give himself time to get to know Billy and find out how different it was to date a shifter from a human. Besides, Niall trusted Val. If Val said it was no different than having a human boyfriend, Niall would trust him.

"Although, of course, there's the bonding," Val continued.

Niall glared at him. "What do you mean?"

"That's the one bit that's different, I guess. You don't bite your boyfriend when you marry him, but you're going to have to do it with Billy."

Niall's stomach churned at the thought. He was nowhere ready to bond or even to think about it. "We'll talk about that when we get to it. It's not going to be anytime soon, though."

Val looked amused. "That's what you think, but I wouldn't be too sure, if I were you. It's easy to fall in love with your mate, much easier than you'd expect, even considering how you felt about Billy until recently."

"I'm not going to rush into this."

"I don't think you could call it rushing, not when it's with your mate. But all right. I'm not going to push you, and I don't think Billy will, either. This is too important to him. I'm curious to see what's going to happen, though."

"I know what's going to happen. Billy and I will date, and we'll get to know each other. Once we do, in a few years, we can start talking about bonding."

"Sure. Keep telling yourself that. I'll be there when you realize you were wrong, and I'll make sure to laugh in your face."

This time, Niall did grab his brush to flick fresh paint at Val's head. "Shut up."

Val was laughing as he shook his head. "This is going to be fun."

Niall wasn't sure that was the case, but for the first time, he was eager to find out what would happen with Billy and if the two of them could genuinely work together as a couple—as *mates*.

"What do you think about this shirt?" Billy asked, turning this way and that in front of the mirror.

"It's the same as the last two shirts you put on, except a different color," Jude drawled.

Billy turned to glare at him. "You're not helping. I need to know if I look good in it."

Jude scrambled into a sitting position. "Of course you look good in it. You'd look good in a trash bag."

Billy rolled his eyes and turned back to the mirror. Jude wasn't wrong, though. He *did* look good in this shirt, and in every other one he'd tried this afternoon. That was why he'd bought them. "Do you think it's good enough for a first date with Niall?"

"Again, he probably wouldn't care if you went wearing a trash bag."

Jude *really* wasn't helping, but then Billy didn't need his help. He knew what he had to do. This wasn't his *first* first date, even though it had been a while since he'd been on one.

He smoothed his shirt down his stomach, still staring at himself and wondering if there was anything else he could do to be appealing. He didn't know if he needed to or if, like Jude had said, Niall wouldn't care even if he wore a trash bag.

"So, what are your plans?" Jude asked.

"I'm going on a date with Niall." Billy was pretty sure he'd told Jude that and that Jude knew that was why he was getting dressed.

"I meant in the future. Will you be moving to Green Hill?"

Billy didn't want to talk about it, especially not right now, but he knew Jude. His best friend wouldn't allow him to hide from making this decision, not now that he was finally moving forward. Besides, he wouldn't be wrong. Billy *had* to make a decision, and he had to make it soon. He had time off work for his honeymoon, but it wouldn't last forever.

"I don't know. I want to, but at the same time, I'm not sure. Niall and I are taking things slow, and I don't know what to make of it."

"You seem pretty happy with him. I mean, all the other dates you went on went well, didn't they?"

Billy finally turned away from the mirror and went to sit on the bed with Jude. "This is the first date."

Jude frowned. "I could have sworn you went on other dates with him. Didn't you grab lunch together the other day?"

"But that wasn't an official date. Niall was at work and only had half an hour to get lunch."

"Okay, what about the ice cream you got Sunday afternoon?"

"Again, not a date. It was just a quick chat over ice cream."

Jude looked at Billy like he was an idiot. "Are you serious? Those were all dates."

"Not really."

"Whatever you want to call them, you spent time with Niall on your own. You talked, whether it was over lunch or ice cream. For me, those are dates, but sure. Let's go with whatever you want."

"I agreed we had to take it slow considering everything, but I'm wondering if maybe we're taking things *too* slow."

Jude tapped his fingertips on his thigh. "What do you mean? What happened during those dates? Or rather, during those non-dates?"

Billy glared, but he answered. "We talked, and Niall kept his distance. It's almost like he's afraid to touch me, even if it's to hold my hand. I don't know if he's even thought about kissing me."

"I'm pretty sure he has."

"But he *hasn't* kissed me. I kissed him a few times the day we talked here, but that's it, and I don't know what to make of all of this. Even though we agreed to go slow, there's slow, and there's glacial slow. That's not what I expected when I agreed to this."

"Then maybe you should talk to him. Tell him that you don't like how things are going and that you want them to change."

"What if he wants me to have decided I want to stay around before he does this, though?"

"How can you make big decisions like that without

knowing what you're getting into? Will you move here even if Niall decides that he doesn't want to be with you after all?"

Billy thought about something like that happening, and it hurt more than he'd expected or than it should. He and Niall barely knew each other, although they'd been talking a lot recently. Just like Billy had expected, Niall was sweet, especially when it came to his family. His eyes lit up when he spoke about them, and it made Billy jealous.

He wanted Niall to care about him as much as he cared about his siblings. He yearned for Niall's eyes to light up the same way when he talked about him. And maybe they did. Maybe when he was with other people, he was free with his affections and the things he said. When he was with Billy, though, he kept himself distant, and Billy didn't know how to break through that or even if he could.

But Jude was right. Billy didn't want to decide whether he should stay in Green Hill only to watch his dreams of being with Niall break down in front of his eyes. Niall wasn't the only reason Billy wanted to move back, but he was a big presence in Billy's life, no matter how recently they'd met. He was Billy's mate, and Billy couldn't ignore that. He didn't want to.

"Talk to him," Jude said. "I know you, and I know you're already worrying about all of this. Obsessing over it isn't going to help you. You have huge decisions to make, and you have to make them soon. You shouldn't decide if you'll move back based on a guy, but Niall isn't just a guy. He's your mate, and that changes a lot. I can't say I understand since I haven't met mine, but I want you to be happy, and I know that right now, that happiness goes through him."

It shouldn't. Even though Niall was Billy's mate, he shouldn't be the reason Billy made decisions. He'd allowed his affection for another man to lead him astray for years, and it had ended with both of them hurt. He shouldn't do the same thing now, even though Niall was his mate.

What did that mean, anyway? Niall was perfect for Billy, or rather, he would be perfect if they had a relationship. They were working toward that, but could they make it work? There was so much more to their relationship and lives than what they were to each other. Billy didn't want to move here only for Niall to decide that maybe it wasn't such a good idea. Right now, it didn't feel like Niall would do something like that, but how was Billy supposed to be sure of it? Niall had admitted he didn't like shifters, or at the very least, that he had trouble understanding them. The fact that he'd accepted he was Billy's mate was a small miracle, and Billy didn't know if he would be so lucky a second time.

Jude sighed. "Stop that," he murmured, leaning closer and kissing Billy's cheek. "I know it's hard, but you need to stop thinking about this for a moment. Go out on your date. Have fun. Talk to Niall and tell him that while you did agree to take things slow, he's taking things too slow, and you don't know what to think of it. I know you're scared of his answer, but I think it's only because you don't know for sure what it's going to be. He's your mate. Do you really think he's going to push you away?"

"I don't know." And that was a problem. Billy had already lost Robin, although that had been entirely his fault. He didn't know if he could stand losing Niall, too.

Who was to say he would lose his mate, though? Jude was right—they should talk, and they should do it as soon as possible before Billy started freaking out and made terrible decisions like running back to the city without talking to Niall. It was hard to resist that urge, but Billy had already run once. He wasn't going to do it twice, not when the first time had ruined everything.

Niall couldn't help but bounce his knee. He kept looking

around, expecting Billy to arrive, but so far, he was nowhere to be seen. That didn't mean much. Billy was always late, from what Niall had been able to see, and while usually that would annoy him, it didn't in this case. It gave him time to think about the date and how things would go.

He and Billy were taking things slow, which meant he'd made sure to stay away as much as possible. They'd talked a lot, but so far, they'd barely even held hands, let alone kissed or done anything more. Niall was pretty sure that if someone could die of blue balls, he would, but the last thing he wanted was to pressure Billy into something he wasn't ready for. Billy had so much to think about and so many decisions to make, and Niall didn't want to influence him or push him in the wrong direction.

Besides, this was their first official date. They'd gone out for lunch and for ice cream a few times, they'd taken walks in the park, and Niall had enjoyed all of it. Tonight felt different, even though he couldn't explain how. Maybe it was more official? He supposed he should have picked Billy up to make it an official date, or maybe Billy could have picked him up, but instead, they'd agreed to meet in front of the restaurant. It made more sense, since Niall had to go home and wash up after work, while Billy lived close to the restaurant since it was in town. Now, though, Niall wished one of them had picked the other up. It wouldn't have given him so much time to worry about how things were going between him and his mate.

It was still strange for him to think that he had a mate, but he was getting used to it. Now that he'd admitted to himself that the only reason he was wary of shifters was that he was an idiot, it was easier to wrap his mind around what was happening. Yes, Billy was a shifter, but it didn't mean he wasn't human. It also didn't mean Niall couldn't trust him, something for which Niall was grateful for.

He truly had been an idiot, hadn't he?

When he heard footsteps come closer, he turned around, smiling. He'd already done this twice, and both times, it hadn't been Billy, and he'd found himself beaming at strangers. It'd made Niall feel like an idiot, but this time, it *was* his mate, and his smile widened. "Hey," he said when Billy reached him.

Billy looked good. He was wearing dress pants and a dress shirt under his jacket, and it made Niall feel underdressed. He wasn't sure he even had a pair of dress pants, so instead, he'd worn his best jeans. The restaurant they'd chosen wasn't elegant or anything like that. This was Green Hill, and while there were a few upscale restaurants, they wouldn't bat an eyelash at seeing Niall wearing jeans. Billy looked good, though, but then, he always did.

And for some reason, he was avoiding looking Niall in the eyes. "Hey. Have you been waiting long?" he asked the wall.

What was going on? "Not really. I arrived about five minutes ago. Do you want to go in, or do you want to take a walk?"

Billy looked confused. "Don't we have a reservation?"

Niall grinned. "In Green Hill? We can go inside and sit down anytime we want. I thought it would be nice to take a walk, though."

Billy looked from the restaurant to the park on the other side of the street. That was one good thing about living in a small town—everything was close by and close to each other. "I guess we should," he finally said.

"We don't have to do it if you don't want to." Something *definitely* was going on, and Niall wanted to ask. Would Billy answer? Since they were taking things so slow, Niall felt like he didn't have a say in Billy's life, but he probably wouldn't even if they were together. Billy was an adult, and he made his own decisions, no matter how Niall felt about that.

He gestured at the sidewalk, and Billy started walking. Niall followed him, wondering how to bring this up. Should he just ask Billy what was going on? Niall wasn't one to play games, and he hoped that if he did, Billy would answer. But maybe they weren't close enough for Billy to. They'd only started dating after all.

"Why are you so distant?" Billy blurted out. From his expression, Niall was pretty sure he hadn't meant to say it out loud, or at the very least, to say it the way he had.

"What do you mean?" he asked cautiously. He didn't want to fight with Billy if he could avoid it.

Billy sighed and rubbed his face. "I shouldn't have asked."

"But you did."

"I was just wondering why you were so distant with me. We've seen each other several times recently, and like Jude pointed out, those were dates, no matter what we call them. You never touched me during any of them, though. I was just wondering why."

Niall blinked. "Because we agreed to take things slow."

Billy threw his hands in the air, clearly frustrated. "I agreed to slow, but this is ridiculous."

Niall had gotten it wrong again. He'd wanted to do everything he could to keep Billy comfortable, which was one of the reasons he'd made sure to keep his distance. He didn't want to push Billy into anything he wasn't ready for, especially since he now knew about Billy's recent past. There was more to it, though, and he realized he should have talked to Billy about it.

"I'm sorry," he said. That was one thing he wanted Billy to be aware of. "It has nothing to do with you, though, not beyond the obvious."

Billy glared. "What does that mean?"

"I'm just not sure what to do with a shifter, and even less with a mate. There's also the fact that I have no idea if you truly are over Robin, and it makes things harder. I know you said you didn't love him and that you haven't been in love with him in a long time, but you were about to marry him, for fuck's sake. How am I supposed to compare to that?"

Billy stopped in the middle of the sidewalk and turned to face Niall. "You're not. You can't compare, or rather, he can't compare to you. You're my *mate*. No matter how important Robin is and was to me, he can never be more important than you."

Billy's words made Niall wonder what would have happened if they'd met after Billy had married Robin. Maybe he shouldn't think about that. The situation he and Billy were in was already complicated enough without *what-ifs*.

"As to what to do with me, what did you do with anyone else you dated?"

"But that's the thing. You're not just a date or a boyfriend. You're my mate, and that's important and changes things. That's what I'm not sure how to deal with. I'm terrified, because I'm falling in love with you, and I don't want to stay away from you, no matter how I acted, but I'm scared. I don't want to get hurt if I lose you."

Niall hadn't meant to say all of that, and especially not in the middle of the sidewalk, but the words were out, and there was no taking them back. He'd exposed how he felt to Billy, and the only thing he could do was hope that Billy wouldn't tear his heart out of his chest and stomp on it. He didn't know what he would do if that happened, although he supposed he might be about to find out.

It was hard to know what Billy was thinking. For now, he was gaping at Niall. Since Niall had made sure to keep his distance until now, it made sense that Billy had no idea what was happening. That was on Niall, and he hoped that he would deal with his feelings for Billy differently in the future. Right now, though, he needed to wait for Billy's answer, and it was the worst kind of waiting.

Billy understood where Niall was coming from. He was terrified, too, and that fear was enough to make him want to hide under the blankets of his childhood bed and refuse to come out. Having his future hinge on one man, even though Niall was his mate, wasn't easy, and the rest of their situation didn't help.

But Niall was falling in love with Billy. He'd said it, even though he looked like he wanted to take the words back. Billy wished he could reassure him, but he was as afraid as Niall looked.

"You don't have to worry about Robin," he started.

"You were going to marry him."

"Because I didn't want to lose my life. I was content, and I didn't think I could be more. I could see myself spending the rest of my life with Robin because I'd already spent so much time with him, and leaving him and everything else behind was scary. I couldn't go through with it, though. No matter how much I wanted to cling to what I had, I didn't want it enough to marry him." He bit his lower lip. "As for the shifter thing, well, there's not much to do. You don't have to deal with me. You just have to accept what I am."

Niall rubbed the back of his neck. "It's not the easiest thing to do when you fainted the only time I saw you in your goat form."

That was Niall's problem? Billy had been terrified there was something more, like maybe that Niall couldn't accept his goat form. He didn't know what he would have done if that had been the case. It was one thing for Niall to be hesitant because he didn't know shifters well, but it would have been different if he hadn't wanted Billy to shift in front of him. If they were going to be together, it would be for a long time.

There was no way Billy could stay in his human form for the rest of his life. Besides, he didn't want to treat shifting as if it was something to be ashamed of. It was who he was, and that was never going to change.

"We can change that," he said.

"What do you mean?"

Billy looked back at the restaurant they were supposed to be eating at. He was hungry, but this was more important, and besides, he was spending time with his mate. That was the only thing that mattered, especially when they were talking about important things. "Can we go to your place?"

Niall looked nonplussed. "You want to go to my house?"

"I wouldn't ask if I didn't. You're not wrong when you say that the only time you saw me in my goat form, I fainted in front of you. We can change that. I can shift and allow you to get used to that form, too. We should probably do that anyway. If we're going to be together—"

"There's no if about it. We *are* going to be together." Niall sounded fierce, but it only lasted for a moment. "Unless you don't want to."

Billy took a risk and stepped closer. He pressed his hand against Niall's chest, smiling at the feeling of Niall's heart beating under his touch. It was beating faster and faster, and it gave Billy a thrill. Niall might not know what to do or how to deal with him, but he wanted him. That was one thing Billy was sure of. "I want you." He had to be honest, even though it was kind of terrifying. "I don't think that's ever going to change."

"It did change with you and Robin." But even though his words were harsh, Niall pressed his hand over Billy's. He linked their fingers together, and they stood there, in the middle of the sidewalk, staring at each other.

"But Robin wasn't my mate," Billy explained. "I know some people don't like the thought of it, but being mates does change things. I'll never get tired of being with you. I'll never fall out of love with you. I'm not saying our relationship will be easy if we decide to have one, but if we work hard, we can be blissfully happy. I could never be that happy with Robin, and no matter how much I told myself that it didn't matter, it does. It makes a difference in whether or not I'll fight for this. I couldn't fight for what I had with Robin. Not once I realized how wrong it was. I can and will fight for what I have with you, though."

Niall squeezed Billy's hand. "Even though so far, we don't have a lot?"

"*So far* is the right word. We haven't allowed ourselves to have more than what we have. We agreed to take things slow, and I don't think it was a mistake, but I do think we took things *too* slow. It hasn't been helpful, and we'll need to change that."

"How are you planning on doing that?"

"By going to your house."

Niall had bought a house a few years ago, and he was fixing it bit by bit. The thought was fascinating, and Billy couldn't wait to see the place. Maybe eventually, he would even move in with Niall. It wasn't Billy's home now, and there wasn't anything of his in it, but that would change. He was sure of it.

"I don't have a problem showing you my place. I just want to be sure it's what you want and that you're not doing it because you think you have to."

Billy didn't know how he could ever have thought that Niall was irritating and a bad person. Well, maybe Niall *was* irritating, but he wasn't bad, no matter how rude and gruff he was. He wanted the best for Billy and for everyone else in his life. He was showing that time and time again, and it made Billy want to take a step forward, to close his eyes and fall and allow himself to trust.

And he did trust Niall, no matter how strange that sounded.

"I'm planning to shift once we get there," he explained. He twisted their hands so they could keep them together as they started walking again. "You didn't have the best experience when I first shifted in front of you, but I can show you that me being a shifter isn't a problem for either of us."

"Will you faint this time, too?"

Billy playfully glared at his mate and knocked their shoulders together. "Only if you freak me out."

"I want to see, then."

Billy was relieved. The next step would be for Niall not to freak out when he saw Billy shift, and for once, Billy was hopeful. Niall's doubts were legitimate, and Billy would work on showing him he shouldn't have them.

Billy had walked to the restaurant, since his mom's apartment was close to Main Street. He was grateful he didn't have to think about his car as he and Niall headed toward Niall's truck. He wanted to focus on Niall, because he felt this would be a big step in their relationship, and he prayed he was right. Maybe it was time for him to stop playing the victim and take his life in hand. He'd allowed himself to be content for years, but now he wanted more.

He wanted Niall.

They were silent as Niall drove them to his house. Billy wished they were bonded so he could know what Niall was feeling, but they weren't, so he could only try to read his mate's expression, which wasn't easy in the darkness.

"You know, you don't have to do anything more than you're already doing," he murmured.

Niall didn't look at Billy, but Billy knew his attention was on him. "You mean be rude?"

Billy smiled. "No. I mean accepting me. Talking to me and getting to know me." Billy hesitated. "I'm nowhere ready to bond. I might be over what was between Robin and me, but I don't want to rush this. You're my mate, and even though I know you're the perfect man for me, it doesn't mean this won't be hard work. I'm ready to do anything I need for us to work, but taking things slow still sounds good."

"Just not *too* slow."

"Yes. I don't want us to stand still. I want us to move forward, slowly but surely."

Niall quickly glanced at Billy. He was smiling, thankfully. "We can do that. I'm relieved I won't have to force myself to stay away from you anymore," he said as he turned into a driveway and stopped the car. "I didn't want to crowd you, but fuck, I've wanted to kiss you since you almost killed me with your car."

Billy glared at him, but Niall was already snapping off the seatbelt and twisting in his seat. "I didn't almost kill you." He reached for Niall, pulling him close as he leaned forward. "But I've wanted to kiss you since then, too."

So he did.

Things were nowhere near perfect, not between them and not in Billy's life, but they were changing, and as Billy kissed his mate, he knew everything would be okay.

CHAPTER SEVEN

Billy jerked when someone hugged him from behind, then relaxed when he realized it could only be one person. He twisted his head around to glare at his mate. "Really?" he asked.

Niall grinned. "What? I just wanted to hug my mate."

The words helped Billy relax even more. "You could have done it from the front, or at least told me it was you. I was about to punch you."

"Would it be that different from trying to kill me with your car?"

Billy huffed. It had become a joke between them, so they were still talking about it, even though it had happened months ago.

By now, Billy had been back in Green Hill for close to a year. In the beginning, it hadn't been easy, and not just because he and Niall were still trying to work things out between them. Leaving all his life behind had been hell and precisely what he'd been trying to avoid by marrying Robin. All of that was behind them now, and he was able to focus on his future rather than his past.

He had a new job, and while he was still living in his mom's apartment, she wasn't anymore. She'd moved in with Niall's father a few months after Billy had moved back, and she was blissfully happy.

Which was why Niall and Billy were at her and Regan's wedding right now.

Billy still had a hard time believing his mom had gotten

married. He was so used to her being a single mom, but it was good to see. He knew Regan would do everything he could to make her happy, which was everything Billy could have hoped for. What his mom did wasn't his business, but it gave him hope.

"Do you think we can have that, too?" Niall asked.

When Billy checked what Niall was looking at, he saw their parents dancing. His mother was gorgeous in a simple white dress, and Regan wasn't so bad himself, looking dapper in his black suit and a white button-down shirt with rolled-up sleeves. He was holding Billy's mom close and whispering something in her ear while she pressed her cheek against his shoulder. They were the picture of happiness.

"We're happy already, aren't we?" Billy asked.

"That's not what I was talking about, but yes, I'm happy with you. I meant the wedding."

Billy hesitated. After he'd left Robin, he'd never thought he would have the opportunity to get married. He hadn't even thought about it when he'd met Niall because they were mates, and mates seldom got married. They didn't have to, not when they bonded. They would be one forever anyway. "You want to marry me?"

Even from his position facing away from Niall, Billy saw his cheeks flush. "Maybe? I know we haven't talked about it and that we don't need it, but I always imagined myself getting married eventually. We don't have to do it if it makes you uncomfortable, though," Niall added in a rush.

Billy took a moment to think about how marriage made him feel. Even though he hadn't expected it, he couldn't deny it gave him a thrill. If he and Niall got married, they would be one in the eyes of both shifters and humans. Billy would be able to wear Niall's ring—to have a sign that he belonged to his mate. Niall wouldn't be able to bite him, so he wouldn't have the scar on his neck to prove it. A ring might be a nice alternative. "I don't hate the idea," he admitted.

"Not anytime soon, though."

"I don't know. A wedding isn't exactly quick to organize, although that depends on what you expect it to be like. I suppose that if you want to marry me in the next few months, we could come up with something."

Niall used his hold on Billy to turn him around so they could face each other. "Shouldn't we bond first?" he asked.

He was gorgeous today. Well, he always was, but this was the first time Billy saw him dressed so neatly, and it made his stomach churn in the best of ways. Niall and his brother had been their father's groomsmen at the wedding, while Shona and Billy had done the same for Billy's mother. Niall had bitched about having to wear a suit, but Billy hoped he would have the chance to see his mate dressed this way again soon.

Maybe even at their own wedding.

"We don't have to bond at all if you want to get married," he said.

Niall frowned. "You don't want to bond with me?"

Billy wouldn't have known how to answer that question only a few months ago, but now, he did. "I do. I've been thinking about it a lot lately, maybe because of the wedding. I was trying to say that we don't have to do both or do them together. We can get married if that's what you want, and bond in a few years. I realize that bonding with a shifter is a lot more serious than a wedding." Because one could divorce their husband, but they couldn't do the same if they bonded with their mates.

Niall was still frowning, and he took his time answering. "I suppose it's a way to do it."

Billy didn't know what Niall was thinking, but he was mostly quiet for the rest of the night. Billy wasn't worried, not the way he would have been a few months ago. By now, he knew that Niall needed time to wrap his mind around things and think about them. He was always quiet when he had to make a big decision, and their conversation about marriage and bonding pointed to that. It made Billy nervous, but not in a bad way.

They managed to have fun anyway. Jude had moved to Green Hill, too, and he looked like he was having the time of his life. He'd already made friends, but then he'd always been able to do that much faster than Billy. Billy was relieved Jude wasn't a part of the old life he'd had to leave behind, and he knew that his best friend's presence had helped a lot when he'd first settled down in his new life. He wouldn't have felt complete without Jude.

By the time the wedding was over, Billy's feet hurt, and he couldn't wait to take his new shoes off. His mom and Regan had disappeared a while ago, but the party hadn't stopped. A lot of people were still dancing, and while Billy was jealous of their energy, he couldn't wait to slip into bed. He was staying at Niall's place tonight, just like he had been for weeks now. He might as well just move in with Niall, but they needed to talk about it first.

He groaned when he finally sat on Niall's bed and took off his shoes, then his socks. "I don't want to wear those things ever again," he grumbled.

"I told you to break them in before you had to spend the entire evening in them," Niall said.

He was in the bathroom, so Billy couldn't see what he was doing, but he could imagine his expression. There was nothing Niall loved more than *I-told-you-sos.*

He rolled his eyes. "You're right. That's what you wanted to hear?"

Niall finally came out of the bathroom. He'd taken off his tie, his jacket, and his belt, as well as his shoes and socks. His shirt was open halfway through, exposing most of his chest.

Billy's mouth went dry. He hoped that the way he reacted at the sight of his partially naked mate would never change. He wanted to feel flustered by it even when he and Niall were old and white-haired.

Niall got to his knees in front of Billy. Billy jerked back, but Niall just reached for his feet, taking one in both his hands and pushing his thumbs into the arch. Billy moaned and reclined back against the bed, closing his eyes. "I don't know what I did to deserve you, but I'm really fucking glad I have you," he murmured.

"I'm going to take that as a compliment," Niall said with humor in his voice.

"You should, because it was."

The foot massage didn't stay innocent for long. Niall's fingers moved upward, stroking the skin of Billy's ankles and legs. Billy still had his pants on, though, so they couldn't do anything else until he stripped.

He didn't have a problem with that.

He pushed up from the bed, ready to get naked, but Niall stayed on his knees. He didn't move, which made Billy frown. "We can just go to sleep if you're too tired," he offered.

"That's not the problem."

"So there *is* a problem?"

Niall rubbed the back of his neck. "Not a problem, no. I just wanted to do something, but I'm not sure how you'll take it."

Billy slowly sat in front of Niall again. "What is it?"

Niall reached into his pocket, and when he took out a small box, Billy knew what he was planning. He held his breath as Niall opened the box and offered it to him.

"I wasn't sure I should do this," Niall said. "I know a lot of shifters don't get married, especially not to their mate."

"Yes," Billy blurted out.

Niall blinked at him. "Yes, they don't get married to their mate?"

"Yes, I'll marry you."

Niall beamed. "You don't have to if you don't want to," he said, ignoring what Billy had just said.

Billy reached out and took the ring from the box. "Try to stop me and see what happens."

Niall laughed. "I think I'm supposed to be the one to put it on your finger."

"Too late. You shouldn't have hesitated." Billy paused and cocked his head. "But since you didn't get to put your ring on my finger, I'll allow you to take my clothes off."

Niall was still laughing. "Thank you. You're so good to me."

"And you better never forget it." Billy didn't think he would ever forget how good Niall was to him, after all.

Thankfully, he didn't have to tell Niall twice. Now that they were engaged — and Billy had a hard time even thinking those words — Niall was more relaxed. He got Billy naked in a matter of moments, but when he reached for his own clothes, Billy shook his head and stopped him. "Keep them on."

Niall arched a brow. "This is what does it for you?"

"*You* are what does it for me. But yes, you in a suit is incredibly sexy, and I want you to fuck me that way."

He didn't have to repeat himself. He stayed right where he was while Niall took the lube out of the nightstand. One glance from Niall was enough for Billy to know his mate didn't want him to move. Niall had to undo his pants to take his cock out and slick it, but it was a sight that made Billy shudder in pleasure. If he'd known he would be so attracted to Niall in a suit, he would have gotten him to wear one months ago.

"Remind me to get you to dress up as often as possible," he said between two groans as Niall prepped him.

Luckily, they were doing this so often that it didn't take

either of them long to be ready to take the other. Niall had fucked Billy just this morning in the shower.

"You won't have to force me if this is what it gets me," Niall said. He slid his fingers from Billy's hole and wrapped them around his cock.

Billy opened his legs and his arms, welcoming Niall inside of him — welcoming him home.

They fit perfectly together, just like always, but there was an added thrill. Niall's clothes brushed against Billy's skin in a maddening sensation as they moved together. His nipples were hard, but his cock was harder. It was impossible to think about anything that wasn't Niall thrusting inside of him, but he still noticed it when Niall reached for his collar and pushed his shirt off one shoulder.

He looked Niall in the eyes. "You're sure?"

"I've never been more sure of anything. We're going to get married. We might as well bond, too."

"You make it sound like I'm forcing you," Billy grumbled. He knew that wasn't the case, though. It was just Niall not thinking about how he said things.

Instead of bickering with him, for once, Billy kept the words in. Bickering with Niall was always fun, but that wasn't what tonight was about. Tonight was about them, about their bond and their wedding. Since Niall had offered, Billy wasn't going to refuse.

He bit down, grinning like a loon at the taste of blood. He still couldn't believe this was happening, that he'd gone from being miserable to being this happy. He became even happier when Niall lowered his face down to his neck. Niall bit down, pain flaring in Billy's shoulder and neck. He'd expected to have to cut himself so Niall could get to his blood, but to his surprise, he felt the bond between them starting to open. Niall had bitten hard enough to break the skin, and he was drinking Billy's blood.

Since there was no way it was enough, Billy reached up. He shifted only one finger, knowing what he had to do even with no one telling him about it. His shifted form normally didn't have claws, but this one time, that was what his finger turned into. He used it to cut the wound open some more when Niall leaned back. Niall didn't even protest, pressing himself closer as he continued thrusting into Billy and drinking his blood.

It was hard to focus, but thankfully, they didn't have to. Billy sucked down another mouthful of Niall's blood just as Niall nailed his prostate with his cock, and pleasure exploded in his body.

It was like a loop. Billy was still coming when he felt Niall stiffen inside of him and his cock pulsing. The pleasure Niall was experiencing hit Billy like a fist to the stomach, and he came again, or at least, he thought he did. He had no idea which feeling was his and which was Niall's, though, and he clung to Niall's shirt, almost tearing it off his body.

It was easier to breathe once Niall flopped to the mattress next to Billy, dragging him along until Billy's body was half on top of his. Billy's ass was tender—as was his neck—but he'd never been happier.

"Is this what sex is going to be like every time we do it from now on?" Niall asked.

Billy groaned. "I sure hope not. I don't think I'd survive it."

Niall snorted. "Please."

Billy cuddled closer. "I don't think it's going to be like this every time, but you could ask Val."

"I don't talk about sex with him, so no. Besides, our normal sex is good. I don't need it to be like this every time."

"So you're saying I'm a great lay?"

Niall kissed the top of Billy's head. "The best, and I'm lucky enough to get you for the rest of my life."

The words had terrified Billy when he'd been about to

marry the wrong person. Now, though, they made him incredibly happy. Instead of being wary and afraid of the future, he couldn't wait to see what it held for him.

YOU MAY ALSO ENJOY THE FOLLOWING FROM eXTASY BOOKS INC:

Baby Steps
Catherine Lievens

Excerpt

God, you're a dick. It's over.

Laurie stared at the text for a moment before dismissing it. He'd expected this to happen anyway. It always did after a while. Instead of answering his now ex-girlfriend, he opened the string of texts between him and Gilbert, his best friend. Natalie just broke up with me.

He leaned against the counter and quickly looked around the coffee shop. No one was waiting for coffee, and the few customers were busy. That meant he didn't have much to do right now, but his boss would still have his ass if he found him texting on the job. What was he supposed to do, though? Stand around waiting for someone to want coffee?

That didn't take long, Gilbert answered. How long were you with her? A week?

Laurie frowned. Two, I think.

A record. What happened?

Laurie hesitated. I'm not sure.

He could almost hear his best friend sigh. Of course you

aren't. I don't know why I asked. Where are you? Do you need me to come over?

Laurie wanted to say yes, but Roger really would kill him if he did. I'm at work, but I'm off in a few hours. Will you pick me up?

Always. Didn't your boss say something about you not texting while you were working?

He's not here.

That doesn't mean he doesn't know you're texting. Gosh, Laurie. You need to start acting like an adult.

Laurie scowled. Why? I'm nineteen.

Exactly. That means you are an adult, even though you don't seem to believe that.

I don't see why I should act like an adult when people don't view me as one. I can't even get a beer at the bar.

I see you don't want to talk, so I'll see you later.

Laurie stared at the screen for a few moments longer, hoping Gilbert would text something else. He was bored, and he wanted his best friend to distract him. Gilbert was gone, though, so Laurie sighed and put his phone away. When he looked up, he found his boss standing in the door that led to the break room, his arms crossed over his chest, glaring.

Laurie beamed at him, then grabbed the nearest towel and started scrubbing the counter. He saw Roger's shoulders slumped, and the man moved closer.

"I don't know what I should do with you," Roger said.

Laurie was still grinning. "Give me a raise?"

"What for? You do half to work the other employees do. I should fire you."

"But you won't." Laurie batted his lashes. He usually dated girls, but he wasn't against using his charms to get himself out of being fired. Besides, his boss was kind of hot. Not Laurie's type, but he was good eye candy.

"Your mother would kill me," Roger said.

Usually, Laurie disliked living in a small town where everyone knew everyone, but he couldn't deny that sometimes, it came in handy. Roger and Laurie's mother had gone to school together, and they were best friends. He would never do anything to hurt her, which included firing her youngest son. Roger didn't know that if Laurie's mother found out how he behaved, she would kick his ass himself, and Laurie wasn't about to tell him. He wasn't a complete idiot, whatever people usually thought.

"Can you at least act as if you're working?" Roger asked. He rubbed the back of his neck, and his arm muscles bulged. Laurie eyed them, wondering how it would feel to be held down in bed.

He shook his head, not wanting to go down that way. "I am." He raised his towel. "See?"

"Go clean the tables."

Laurie beamed and walked around the counter. He'd won, just like always. It was starting to get boring, but he didn't know what else to do.

He supposed he could look into college, but he wasn't one for books and studying. That was one of the reasons people thought he was an idiot. The other was that he was the youngest of seven brothers, so everyone tended to look at him like a child anyway, even though he wasn't anymore. Tell that to his brothers and his parents, though.

Laurie had stopped trying to convince them he was worthy. He'd decided just to do what he wanted in life, which right now, was working at the shop. It would change eventually, although he didn't know what he would do when it did. He liked his job, even though he didn't do much — or maybe because of that.

That didn't mean he could see himself do this for the rest of his life. He was nineteen, and this was a nice first job, but unless Laurie was planning on buying the shop, he had bigger plans for himself. What those plans were, he had no idea, but he would find out sooner or later. In the meantime, he promised himself he would have fun, and he had every intention of keeping that promise.

He softly snorted, making a girl sitting two tables down look at him. He grinned, and she smiled back. He didn't want to think about how he never kept promises, even the ones he made to himself. His mother already bothered him enough about it, and while he couldn't avoid her lectures, he could avoid lecturing himself, especially at work.

He moved toward the girl. "Hi there. Can I get you anything else?" he said, tilting his chin toward her coffee.

"I don't know. Do you think you can sit with me if I get another coffee?"

"Of course."

"Won't your boss get angry?"

"He's a big teddy bear, so don't worry about that. What did you get again? I'll grab you a second one and something for me."

If Laurie was lucky, he would end the day with a girlfriend, and it wouldn't be Natalie.

Roger looked desperate while Laurie walked around the counter to make two coffees, but thankfully, he didn't say anything. Laurie knew he was pushing maybe too much and that he would have to change something, but he wasn't ready for that yet.

Everyone looked at him and saw a child. If that was what they wanted, it was what he was going to give them.

By the time the girl—Sarah—left the coffee shop, Laurie had her number saved in his phone. They weren't dating yet, but that only was because she wasn't sure when she would have the time to go out with him. She was in college, and it was a lot of work, which was one of the reasons Laurie had no intention of ever going. He already had enough brainiacs in his family. He didn't need to add to it.

"I need you in the stockroom," Roger said when Laurie was done cleaning the table.

"Why? I'd rather work here."

"I know, which is why I'm sending you back. And if you were wondering, I'm your boss, and I'm the one who gives orders here. Unless you're planning on buying the shop from me, you're supposed to obey."

Laurie smiled. "I'm aware you're the boss." He gave Roger an impressed once over, smiling even wider when Roger's cheeks flushed.

"Stop trying to flirt with me. I know you're not into me, and nothing you do or say will change that," Roger snapped. He sucked in a breath. "Just go."

Laurie didn't mind. At least in the stockroom, he could sit down and not look like he was supposed to be busy.

By the time Laurie's work day was over, he'd texted back and forth with Sarah, and he was pretty sure they would have their first date this week, or maybe the next. It was a bit too far away for him, but it wasn't like he couldn't find someone else if he wanted to. As long as they were nothing like Natalie, he didn't really care who he dated.

His phone rang just as he stepped out of the shop. He waved at Gilbert, who was sitting in his car waiting for him, and rushed toward him as he answered. "Yes?" He hoped it was Sarah, but he should have checked first.

"Finally. I was sure you were dead in a ditch somewhere," his mother drawled.

Laurie huffed as he slid into the car. "You're not funny, Mom. What do you want?"

"Just to know if you're coming over for dinner."

"I don't know. I just got off work, and I need to go home. I don't like smelling of coffee for the rest of the evening."

"You should still have time to come over for dinner, though. I'll be waiting for you."

"I didn't say I was coming!" It was too late. She'd already hung up, and he glared at his phone until the screen turned black.

"We should go," Gilbert said.

"I thought you were on my side."

"I am. I also love your mom, though."

"I have no idea why," Laurie grumbled. But he did. Gilbert

had lost his mom when he was a teenager, and he'd pretty much lived with Laurie and his family after that. "Fine," Laurie added. "We can go." He suspected he would regret this, but Gilbert was one of the few people he truly cared about, and he wanted his best friend to be happy. If having dinner with his family made that happen, then Laurie would suffer through it.

ABOUT THE AUTHOR

Catherine is the creator of several series, most of them paranormal, including the Whitedell Pride Series and the Gillham Pack Series. While she graduated in translation, she decided to go the writer's way because it was more fun to create her own stories and characters.

She's been living in Italy for more than twenty years, but she's a daughter of the North—Belgium to be precise—and she misses it so much that she's already planning to move back.

She loves pizza—probably too much—her son, her pets, and of course, books. She sneaks some reading time into her schedule every time she has five minutes free from writing, demands from her various pets and son, and lastly, housework.

Connect with her:

lievens.catherine@gmail.com
BookBub: https://www.bookbub.com/authors/catherine-lievens
Website: https://authorcatherinelievens.com/
Facebook: https://www.facebook.com/catherine.lievens.9
Facebook Group: https://www.facebook.com/groups/411788002341528/
Twitter: https://twitter.com/authorCLievens
Newsletter: http://eepurl.com/c-uvKn